CALAMITY @ THE CARWASH

by

Sharon Rose

For information, email **Cozy Cat Press**, cozycatpress@aol.com or visit our website at: www.cozycatpress.com

COZY CAT
PRESS

ISBN: 978-0-9881943-0-4
Printed in the United States of America
Cover design by Karri Klawiter
http://artbykarri.com/e-book-print-cover-art-design/

1   2   3   4   5   6   7   8   9   10

This book is dedicated to every friend and family member who read my unpublished work and who was brutally honest with me. And, thank all of you for telling me it was perfect!

CHAPTER ONE

Flori and I were enjoying our second cup of coffee when we heard the sirens whizzing past. Well, it was only one patrol car but it sounded like five or six. That's because our two deputies, Jim and Scully, decided to attach a few extra bells and whistles. At first, Sheriff Smee was upset but because everyone in town thought it was a real blast, he left them. I'm quite sure he not only secretly enjoys the loud noise, he relishes a bit of attention now and again too. Perhaps that's because he will retire soon and wants to go out with some sort of bang.

It had started out as another quiet Thursday afternoon; after all, whatever happens on a Thursday? The temperature had climbed to unfathomable heights the whole week so Flori and I sat in front of the small but reliable air conditioner that I have stuck in the corner of one of my windows with plywood surrounding it. It might not be pretty but the window is on the west wall and faces the east side of Mildred Norton's Flower Shop. Gwen has no windows on that side of her building and the only thing between us is a narrow well-worn path with tall weeds growing along both sides.

The small flower shop belonged to Gwen's mom, Mildred Norton, but she never had the heart to put up a new sign. I'd suggested *Gwen Friesen's Fine Flora*, which I thought had a bit of zip to it and would match nicely with my sign; however, for some reason she felt that she was being unfaithful to her birthright. I felt that

I was still carrying on the Wickles' legacy so it didn't bother me at all to change my store's name from *Wickle's Food Fair* to *Mable's Fables and Things*.

I was definitely not going to continue selling groceries so before my father died, I gradually started installing my own merchandise. For example, I cleared out one section of canned goods and replaced them with new and used books. Father made one last visit to the store and when he saw the shelves, he shook his head. I'm sure I saw a tear or two trickle down his cheeks. He never came back the last month but gave me his blessing so I ripped out the ancient freezer and the bins where he kept the sugar and flour. I brought in racks of cards for all occasions, fancy boxes of notepaper and a wide variety of salt and peppershakers, souvenirs, collectable cups and saucers and enough knickknacks to make your head swirl.

"Where do you think Reg is off to?" Flori asked as she drained her cup. Her bright red hair flopped up and down in time with each blast coming from the a/c. Every few minutes she faced the air conditioner head-on to free some hair from her mouth and eyes. The heat and humidity hadn't been kind to Flori and her hairdo. Two days before she'd come into the store sporting her new 'do' and the sight of it left me speechless and believe me, not much does that anymore. I was used to the bright red color. She'd decided to do that when she turned fifty. Now that she was over sixty, it seemed she was getting even more adventuresome. The usual curly hair was now as straight as a board with the front sides comin' down to her chin and the back cut up high in the nape of her neck. In my opinion, it did nothing for her but then again, who was I to judge? I've had my silver hair cut in the same short style since 1960. I doubt hairdressers even call it a 'do' anymore - more like a 'past do.'

"I don't know but whatever it is, he seems to think it's worth sounding off with the sirens. At least, it will wake the town up. This heat is making everyone miserable and cranky. Can you guess who came into the store yesterday and was really nice to me?"

"I thought you said everyone was miserable and cranky?"

"They are, that's why this is so phenomenal – so, can you guess?"

Flori picked a strand of hair out of her eye and tried hooking it behind her ear. "If everyone is cranky, how can I guess who's nice?"

"Esther Flynn."

Flori gasped. "Esther was nice to you? Why? She's never nice to you."

I shook my head. "I know. Go figure. Everyone else is ready to commit murder in this heat and Esther is not only as cool as a cucumber, she was actually civilized."

We both muttered to ourselves for a few seconds. Flori said something about the Devil liking it hot too but because we were too exhausted from the heat, we didn't try to pursue it. Besides, the wind from the air conditioner kept blowing our words away.

Esther Flynn, by the way, is my nemesis. This is not something new; this is something that has been in the making for the past fifty or so years. In other words, my life would be as close to perfect as you can come if it weren't for Esther. Why everyone else in Parson's Cove was crabby and Esther, for the first time in her life, was almost pleasant was a mystery I wasn't about to try to solve. As they say, let sleeping dogs lie – especially when it's over a hundred degrees in the shade.

It wasn't until several hours later that I found out the reason for the sirens: Melanie Bernstein found Bernie, her husband, dead on the beach. His head and shoulders were the only part not submerged in the water. Perhaps it could've passed as a drowning except for the large bashing he'd received on the back of his head. It happened right behind the Parson's Cove Car Wash. Melanie, it seems, was waiting in the car while he went to make change. She waited for two hours with the car running and the air conditioner on before deciding there must have been some reason for his not returning.

Chapter Two

It was after five when I heard the news. I'd left the store about four because I knew there wouldn't be any customers. I couldn't imagine a last minute rush for any of my nonessentials. It's not as if I had any air conditioners or electric fans in stock. I don't even have ice cubes. Not a soul had entered through those doors all day except for Flori. Who, because she's my best friend, comes in every day – rain, snow, sleet or heat – and then there was Merlin Cowel, who walked across the street from the pharmacy to deliver my prescription. I don't know why Merlin thought he had to deliver the little tube of salve that Doc Fritz insisted I needed for a rash on my arm. I think Merlin was curious and thought I'd tell him where my itch was. He left, disappointed.

It was nothing short of a miracle that I even heard about Bernie as quickly as I did because the last thing I felt like doing when I got home was answering the phone. I only did because I knew it was Flori and if I didn't answer, she'd leave four or five messages on my machine. If I didn't call back immediately, she'd be running over to see what had happened to me. Or, worse yet, she would send Jake over. I can live without Jake. Flori, who's been married to him for over forty years, cannot. That woman has more love in her heart than Mother Theresa. She loves me unconditionally and at the same time puts up with Jake and all of her kids and her grandkids. I don't know how she does it. I have seven cats and they drive me nearly insane. I'm not even sure of any of their names most of the time.

Not that I planned to have seven cats. Someone (Flori) coaxed me into taking one kitten. I was hoping that this one kitten (named Phil after Prince Philip in England) would keep mice out of my house. Not that it's a problem but sometimes in the fall, the field mice seem to think it would be rather pleasant to winter in my house. I suppose it's to them like a Mexican vacation is to us humans. Anyway, to make a long story short, Phil turned out to be Phyllis and she had five kittens. That, I know, makes only six cats. The old tomcat, however, which was to blame for the sordid affair started creeping around so I seized him and did the unthinkable - 'he' is now an 'it'- as are the other six.

(I'm sorry but I have to clear this up at the beginning because I don't want you thinking that I'm a crazy cat woman. When they were small, they were too cute to give away and when they got older, no one wanted them. After that, I couldn't bear to, you know ... put them to 'sleep.')

"Mabel," Flori screamed in my ear. I hadn't even had time to say hello. "Bernie Bernstein is dead. Melanie found him in the lake. Somebody murdered him."

There was silence because my brain couldn't kick into gear.

"Mabel," she screamed again. "Are you there? Didn't you hear me? Bernie Bernstein is dead. Melanie found him in the lake. Somebody murdered him." The last three sentences, she spoke slowly and deliberately - and at full volume.

"Flori, I heard you the first time. What do you mean - Bernie is dead? Who would want to kill Bernie? There must be some mistake. If Melanie found him in the lake, he probably drowned. Who told you this anyway? Was it Jake?"

I asked this because Jake can get stories mixed up. If I had more time, I could give many examples.

"Mabel." Flori only uses this voice on certain occasions. It means, shut up, Mabel. "Yes, Jake did tell me but he got it from a very reliable source."

"Who? Amos?" (Amos Grimm is a lovely man except that he's usually three sheets to the wind by nine in the morning.)

"Oh, for Pete's sake, it wasn't Amos. I'll have you know, Miss Smarty Pants, it was from Reg Smee himself."

Since Reg Smee happens to be a dedicated Sheriff who never lies about a crime, I guess I could accept it as truth.

"Okay, what else do you know, Flori? Why does Reg think it's murder?"

"Because apparently someone hit Bernie on the head and then tried dumping him in the lake. Poor Melanie, she's in the hospital now in shock. I'm thinking I should take her some chicken soup or something."

"Flori, I don't think you take chicken soup to someone in shock. The thought is very ... well, thoughtful, but Melanie would probably be better off with a strong prescription drug."

She sighed. "You're probably right. I don't know. It's so hard to believe, isn't it? I mean, why would anyone want to hit Bernie on the head?"

"Maybe nobody did. What if he fell and hit his head and then slid down into the lake? I'm sure that could easily happen."

"Except," Flori said, speaking as if to a ten year old. "That is not what happened. Someone definitely hit Bernie on the back of the head."

"On the back of the head? With what?"

"I don't know, Mabel. I don't think Reg told Jake everything." She sighed. "I hate violence. You know how I hate it." She gasped and I knew she was off on a crying binge. I waited patiently. After several minutes of loud weeping, she stopped, blew her nose, hiccoughed three times, and then resumed talking. "Now who would want to murder Bernie Bernstein? I can't think of a single soul who would want to hurt such a sweet man."

"What about Melanie? The first suspect is usually the person's mate. Maybe she didn't think he was such a sweet man. You never know, Flori. You never know what goes on behind closed doors. Where was she when all this murdering was going on?"

I heard Flori gasping. It's very hard for her to get her head around anything that's evil or sometimes even slightly evil. If there is a murder, in Flori's mind it has to be an accident or a demented stranger who did the deed – someone who escaped from the depths of Hades. It makes her cringe to think she might have walked on the same sidewalk as a killer - even a shoplifter for that matter.

"That's the most terrible thing to say, Mabel. Obviously, it was a stranger who was waiting by the carwash to hit him on the head and steal his money. No one in Parson's Cove would do such a thing. It was someone from the city. It had to be. Maybe an escaped convict."

"The carwash? What was Bernie doing at the carwash?"

"They were obviously there to get their car washed."

"By 'they,' do you mean Bernie and someone else?"

"Of course, Melanie was with him. Reg said that Bernie went out get change from that coin machine on the side of the building and he never came back. Melanie waited and waited. In fact, she waited for two hours and he never returned so she went to look for him. And, there he was, Mabel - dead." With that, she burst into tears again.

I waited for what seemed like two hours too. Finally, the wailing ceased, along with all the other noises that accompany her cries.

"Doesn't it seem strange that Melanie sat in the car for two hours and never bothered to get out and look for her husband?" I continued.

"Mabel, we don't have all the details. If you are in your 'detective' mood, I'm not talking to you. I thought I was being a good friend by filling you in on what I do know. I did not phone to ask you to solve a murder case. And trust me, Reg is not asking for your help either."

"How do you know that, Flori?"

"Because he warned me not to call you but I knew he couldn't arrest me for doing it so I disobeyed the Law. I hope you're pleased with that. Now you can just leave it alone and let the police do their job. I'll come by the shop with some cinnamon buns tomorrow. I'll see you then and I don't want to talk about Bernie Bernstein anymore. Good night, Mabel." With that, my best friend hung up.

And with that, I dug out my hidden bottle of gin, poured a generous portion and hightailed it upstairs to bed to make a list of suspects.

Chapter Three

I woke up early the next morning for several reasons. Firstly, although the air conditioner in my bedroom window was purring away like a kitten and sounding as if it was working its little heart out, it was all a farce. The only thing that it was pouring into my bedroom was hot air from outside. Secondly, smelly sweat covered my entire body. There isn't a pleasant way to describe it. Thirdly, there were seven cats sitting on my bed. None of them looked very happy. I could almost put up with the first two but having seven over heated cats in the house is too much for any human body to endure.

The moment I opened my eyes, they all started complaining.

"What are you nattering about?" I said, without lifting my head off the pillow. "Bernie Bernstein got clipped on the head and is dead. So, don't start telling me what a hard life you have."

I'm not sure if they understood or not but as soon as I said the word 'dead' they all jumped off the bed and headed for downstairs and their food dishes.

I glanced over at the clock and sighed. It wasn't even six yet. I lifted the wet sheet off and lay spread-eagle. The hot air from the air conditioner didn't even ruffle my cotton nightgown; it clung to me like paste. If I went out to pick up the newspaper wearing this garment, Reg would arrest me for indecent exposure.

I had no energy to move but from the bowels of my kitchen came the cries of my ravenous felines so I knew

I'd have to get up. There would be no peace until I did. I rolled out of bed, almost taking the wet sheets with me, and went over to shut off the air conditioner. There was no way this old thing would be fixable so I knew what that meant - I'd have to either put out for a new unit or start sleeping in my cellar.

My cellar was a hole in the ground until I had some cement walls and a floor poured about thirty years ago. Everyone in the neighborhood did the same thing. We had old houses but we wanted to have nice dry sweet smelling basements with laundry rooms and recreation rooms. Perhaps, even a spare bedroom for guests. Well, now we have cellars with cement walls and floors but that's all. They are still dark, damp and moldy. I had Jake and one of his boys lug my washer and dryer down there as soon as the cement dried. Now, I use the Laundromat because, even though I haven't checked in several years, I'm sure my appliances have literally disintegrated into a pile of rust bunnies.

Even in the heat, my cats still kept up their appetites. Me? I could barely wash down an apple muffin with my cup of coffee. After gorging themselves for several minutes, they rushed to the backdoor in one accord and stood there with their tails in the air, waiting for me to let them out. As soon as I walked toward them, there was a chorus of cheers. I opened the door, they felt the blast of hot air, looked at me as if I was to blame for the heat and then they scattered through the house in all directions.

"Okay," I yelled at them. "You want to stay in and use your litter box all day, that's up to you, but one of these days I'm going to train you to clean it out yourselves and then you'll be sorry."

You would think that after all this time I'd learn but I never do. Cats don't care how much you threaten;

they're going to do whatever they want anyway. Sometimes it just feels good to get if off your chest.

I managed to peel my nightclothes off, have a cool shower, and get to the shop before seven thirty. My store doesn't open until 9:00 but the air conditioner works.

It was exactly 9:02 when Flori rushed in telling me that Melanie Bernstein was in jail, arrested for murdering her husband.

Chapter Four

"But I don't understand," I said for about the fourth time. "What proof do they have that Melanie killed Bernie?"

Flori, with her tear-stained face and swollen red eyes, said, "Well, you're the one who thought she was guilty in the beginning so why are you surprised?"

"I know I said that, Flori, but I don't think I really believed it to be true. They have to have a motive and proof."

"I told you; Bernie took out a life insurance policy just a few weeks ago. Apparently, they were in big trouble financially. There's your proof and motive." She buried her nose back into the soppy blob of wet tissues.

"I don't care how much financial trouble they were in, Flori, no woman is stupid enough to go out almost immediately after getting the insurance, kill her husband, and think she can get away with it. Melanie might not be the sharpest knife in the drawer but even she has more sense than that. They must have something else on her."

Flori didn't answer - she simply reached over, pulled out about six more tissues and proceeded to drown her sorrow in them. When it comes to crying, or laughing for that matter, Flori overflows. I've found that it's better to be patient and wait; eventually, she dries up.

While waiting, I poured another cup of coffee and thought about Bernie and Melanie Bernstein. I remembered when Melanie was born. She was probably in her early forties now. Flori used to babysit her once in awhile when her parents went out for supper or to a wedding or something like that. Not much ever goes on in Parson's Cove and back then, there was less. Flori babysat for quite a few people when we were teenagers. No one ever asked me but Flori always said that was because I was an only child and parents didn't think I'd be good at it. I'm glad they thought that because I wasn't very keen on children. Even now, I prefer watching them from afar.

Bernie arrived in Parson's Cove when Melanie was finishing high school. He was like a small town beach bum – happy to work just enough to eat and pay his rent. He was in his twenties then and Melanie used to follow him everywhere. Except when she was in classes, of course, but she apparently missed a few of those too. On one such occasion, her father caught the two of them skinny-dipping in a lonely spot on the lake. Daddy made sure they were standing at the altar almost before she got her clothes back on.

They never had any children but Melanie seemed content to have Bernie as her pet. They went everywhere together. Probably about twenty years ago, they started up their own cleaning business. B & M Cleaners. It caused a few snickers but they didn't seem to catch on so the jokes dwindled down to nothing. Once in awhile, even now, some kid will paint over the '&' on their truck. Personally, I thought they were doing very well. At least, they charged enough for their services. Once, I thought I'd splurge and get my shop professionally cleaned. They gave me a quote and I almost fainted. I told Bernie I didn't want them building me a completely new store; I just wanted my little space cleaned. Neither one of them talked to me for about a year after that.

After snorting her last snort, Flori said, "What about fingerprints? Maybe her prints were on whatever she used to hit him. I'm sure she didn't mean to kill the man. I mean, I'd love to hit Jake over the head sometimes but I wouldn't hit him hard enough to do any real damage."

"Flori, it will take days to check something for fingerprints. We're out in the boonies here and no lab in the city is going to do a rush job for Sheriff Smee, you can be sure of that. No, Reg wouldn't arrest her unless he had some real proof. Maybe I should give Reg a call."

"Are you crazy? That's the last thing you should do. If you intend to find out the details, which I'm sure you are, you'd better do it very discreetly. And, when you do, Mabel, you make sure that I am not involved in any way." She glanced up at the Coca-Cola clock I have above the door. "Oh my, I'd better get back home before Jake comes back for breakfast."

"What do you mean, before Jake gets home? And, by the way, I noticed you forgot the cinnamon buns."

Flori's face turned from chalk to crimson.

"Oh, for Pete's sake, I completely forgot about those buns. I was rushing to get over here so I could get back real quick and I left them on the counter. I am so sorry, Mabel. After I feed Jake, I'll come back with the buns."

She jumped off the chair as daintily as a woman her size can and almost ran to the door.

Flori comes by her weight honestly; she cooks and bakes with real butter, real cream, and real sugar. Of course, I do too but somehow even with all my trying, I can't ever reach my goal of a hundred and ten. It's a good thing I'm barely over five feet tall.

Before she lit out, I called, "Why is Jake so late for his breakfast?"

"Because he's trying to get more information about the murder." Then, realizing what she'd said, she had the decency to blush and say, "Not that he'll find much out. You know the men at Main Street Café don't gossip like we do, Mabel."

She closed the door before I could tell her that she'd better pass that information on if she knew what was good for her. Also, if she thought those old fellows didn't gossip more than we women did, Flori didn't know beans. Delores, who's worked there for years, says some of the things they say about their so-called friends behind their back would curl your hair. She told me once never to confide in any man in Parson's Cove who was over fifty. Unless, of course, I wanted everyone in town to find out the next day.

However, knowing Flori, she would feel so guilty about forgetting to bring the cinnamon buns over that it would be much easier to pry information out of her. That is, if Jake had any.

Chapter Five

A few customers popped in that morning – if you can call two, a few. For the most part, both of them came not to buy but to find out if I knew anything about Melanie's arrest. It was probably a good thing at that point in time that I didn't know anything so I didn't have to lie. I guess the word spread that I was out of the loop so no one else bothered coming in.

I had no idea what happened to Flori and her cinnamon buns. She didn't even phone which is very unlike her.

By ten o'clock, I gave Reg a call because I'd thought of a good ruse. Scully answered and told me to 'hold.'

"Reg," I said, after waiting eleven minutes for him to come to the phone, "I'll make this clear right off the bat - I don't want any information about the murder. But someone told me that Melanie Bernstein was in a cell. Since I happen to know how terrifying that can be, I was wondering if I should bring over some fresh apple muffins and coffee for her."

I'd spent a night in the hoosegow myself (it was a case of mistaken identity) and I'm well known for my muffins and coffee so I thought this would come across as a natural request.

Apparently, not.

"Well, Mabel, since you obviously know I have Melanie Bernstein incarcerated and I'm sure you know that I'm conducting an investigation, am I correct in assuming you know that I'm very busy?"

"Oh I do know that, Sheriff Smee. I was thinking that if this is Melanie's first arrest though, she might need someone to talk to. And, as you know, everyone loves my coffee and muffins. In fact, I could bring some over for you and the boys too. Would you like that?"

It has to be a freezing day in hell when Reg refuses one of my muffins.

Apparently, not.

"No, I would not like that. I don't want you within a hundred yards of this place. You got that, Mabel? If I so much as see you hiding behind a bush across the street, I'll lock you up with Melanie myself."

I guess he realized then that he was making an opening for me so he changed his tactics and said, "I'll put you in with her and plaster duct tape over both your mouths."

Before I could make a rebuttal, he hung up. Obviously, I was not going to get any info from him. At least, not for the time being.

Five minutes later Flori burst through the door. The heat and humidity were doing their number on her again. Perspiration dripped from her hairline, down her cheeks, her neck and made a narrow river, ending up somewhere between her ample bosoms. Even her flowery lime green and turquoise sundress which usually billows out like a golden aspen tree, hung straight down like a weeping willow. She did not carry any cinnamon buns in her hands either.

Before saying a word, she rushed up to the air conditioner, closed her eyes, and spread her hands up to the sky. I hope it's a sight I never witness again.

"Flori," I said. "Put your arms down." I ran into the back room and proceeded to spray air freshener into the room.

"Oh for Pete's sake, I don't smell."

"No one can smell their own smell," I said. "How come you're so late? And, the cinnamon buns? I don't see them anywhere either."

"Mabel," she said. "I can't think of everything. There are so many things happening. I told Jake today that I want to move away - anywhere to get away from Parson's Cove."

"I think that's a bit drastic, especially for you. You know you'd never leave your kids or me for anything."

"You haven't heard?"

"Heard what?"

"About Murray?"

"What about Murray?"

"Well, you know that Murray McFerguson is ... or, I should say, *was* Bernie's fishing buddy, right?"

"Right. An unlikely pair but it's true. Aren't Erma and Melanie friends too?"

"Sort of." A trace of sadness crossed her face. "I think it's so wonderful when two couples can be friends." She looked at me with puppy dog eyes. "Wouldn't it be wonderful if you were married and the four of us could do things together?"

"That, Flori, is never going to happen." There is no way I would even consider marrying anyone who chummed with Jake Flanders. Of course, I would never tell my best friend that. I got up and went into the back room to fetch two bottles of water out of the small fridge.

"Here." I handed one to her. "It's too hot for coffee. Maybe if we had cinnamon buns..."

We both took a slug of water.

"So, what's all the excitement about? What about Murray and Erma?" I asked.

Flori's eyes started to water. "Oh Mabel, I was sure you'd heard. I thought some of your customers would've told you."

"Told me what? Were Murray and Erma murdered too?"

Flori's eyes bulged. "Oh my lord, no. It's nothing like that. But it's bad, Mabel; it's very sad." She shook her head. "To think that Murray would lose one friend and then another, on the same day. It's just too sad."

"Flori." Sometimes I want to strangle that woman. "Who else died? What other friend of his, died? Quit talking in circles."

At that, Flori burst into tears but in between the sobs, I could make out a name. Biscuit.

"Biscuit? What kind of name is that? He had a friend named Biscuit?" It sounded more like a racehorse to me.

Flori nodded while wiping her nose. She'd already worn out the tissues she'd stuffed down the front of her bra so I handed her about ten more from a box I have on the counter. I should write her name on it.

She stopped sniffling long enough to say, "Biscuit was the name of his old basset hound. Remember him, Mabel? That old dog went everywhere with him."

"So, Flori, are you telling me that we're sitting here, sobbing our hearts out because Murray's old basset hound died or are we weeping because his fishing buddy was murdered?"

Flori's bloodshot eyes stared at me. "We're crying for both. It's not right for a human to be hit over the head and killed with a brick anymore than it's right for an old basset hound to be hit over the head and killed with a brick."

It was my turn to stare at her. "The same brick?"

She nodded. I handed her the tissue box.

Chapter Six

It was time for me to start doing some serious investigating. I knew that Reg wouldn't come for my help until he was forced to call in cops from the city. When they descend on Parson's Cove, he and his two deputies skedaddle out of the way. Meanwhile, where would I start?

I had to find out why Reg arrested Melanie. Was she in such a murdering mood that she would kill Murray's dog and then, Bernie? Or, was it the other way round? Did she kill Bernie and then take her anger out on that dog? If I remembered correctly, that old hound was too lazy to chase a cat so why would anyone get riled up enough to kill it? Reg, even though I sometimes belittle his detective skills, I do it in a very loving way. He does pretty well for an aging ex-traffic cop. Besides, I honestly think we work quite well together.

I was home now and sweltering in my kitchen. The cats were out carrying on their own adventures. I filled them up with nutritious dry cat food before I let them out so hopefully, they weren't digging into the garbage bin behind Main Street Café again. It isn't that I mind them eating garbage. It's just that it gives our family a very bad reputation. People think I don't feed them.

Well, if Reg wasn't going to fill me in and it didn't seem like Flori had much to share from Jake's empty repertoire, I'd have to move on my own. I knew my first stop.

Let me tell you about my friend, Charlie Thompson. To most people in Parson's Cove, Charlie is slightly on the odd side. Some think of him as being 'slow.' You know – retarded, although no one ever comes right out and says that word. To the most open-minded residents, he's 'different.' To me, Charlie is smarter than most of them put together are. He sits in front of the town library, day in and day out. Winter, spring, summer and fall. He wears the same denim overalls with the same plaid shirts all year round. In winter, I'm sure he must have layers and layers on. I'm always afraid that he'll freeze to death on that bench and we'll have to look at him all winter until the spring thaw. Somehow, he manages to survive. That, of course, isn't what makes him smart – although he obviously saves tons of money on clothing. The smart thing is that he minds his own business and doesn't talk to anyone, except me – occasionally. Charlie is very selective in choosing his friends.

Charlie came to Parson's Cove as a child with his parents. Well, we called them his parents but gossip had it that they were his grandparents, raising their daughter's illegitimate child. You know what small town gossip is like. They were older and when they died, they left Charlie for the town of Parson's Cove to look after. Several families took him in but he never stayed long. I guess the silence got to them. Finally, he was old enough to manage on his own so some of the townsmen fixed up an old house towards the end of Main Street and that's been his home ever since. Main Street dwindles down from stores, to a gas station, to several houses including Charlie's shack, to two empty lots; and then, to a narrow two-lane highway surrounded by forest that leads to more exciting places.

It was close to eight and there was a slight breeze so it was quite a pleasant walk to the library. Down from the library on the other side of Main Street, I can see my own little shop. Main Street Café is next to the library. It's actually quite a boring street. The only thing that's really going for Parson's Cove and probably the only reason some people stay here is the lake. In summer, it's wonderful for swimming, camping and fishing and in the winter when the ice freezes over, hoards of city dwellers come in with their chain saws and go ice fishing. By the time they leave, they're mostly half-frozen and half-drunk. Jake, included.

"Charlie," I said, as I plunked down beside him. I have to watch my approach. Sometimes I must admit, he doesn't talk even to me, his best friend. "Charlie," I repeated, "how are you today?"

Charlie just stared out at the open sky.

"It's a beautiful sunset, isn't it?"

I was drawing a blank.

"So, what were you up to today? Did you hear that Bernie Bernstein died?"

Nothing.

"Did you hear that Bernie Bernstein was murdered and Melanie is in prison, accused of murdering him?"

Finally, there was a twitch in his right cheek. Charlie's cheeks, by the way, are plump. He's a big man and I don't know what he eats but I have a feeling it isn't always fruits and vegetables. If he didn't wander the streets at night, he'd never get any exercise. I have no idea when he sleeps. Well, sometimes he dozes on the bench but that's all I've ever seen. I was inside his little shack once. They say I'm the only woman ever to get inside. It was so clean and tidy that it put my place to shame - and probably most of the houses in town. This shows there are sides to Charlie that people never see.

"Do you know anything about it, Charlie? Did you happen to see anything?"

Charlie started rocking back and forth. This means he's getting nervous but it also means that he knows something.

"You can tell me. You know that I can keep a secret."

"I know, Mabel. It's a mystery though."

"What's a mystery? You mean Melanie killing Bernie?"

He continued his rocking. "No. Other things."

"What other things, Charlie?"

"I don't know. They are a mystery. That's what I said."

He shook his head and started to hum. Drats! That means he's finished talking. I always make sure that I never put any pressure on him. When he's ready, he'll tell me. It tests my patience. This is probably a good thing because I don't have much of it.

I walked across the street and past my shop. Sometimes I like to do this and pretend that I'm visiting Parson's Cove for the first time. If I were a stranger in town, would I be inclined to shop at *Mabel's Fables and Things*?

Probably not. I really don't go in for knickknacks myself.

Well, I didn't get any info from Charlie but he did tell me something. Charlie has a sixth sense when it comes to mysteries. Obviously, something else was going on in our town and it was happening in secret in the dead of the night. Let's hope that only the night was 'dead.'

Chapter Seven

A north wind crept into Parson's Cove and by morning the temperature in my house went from eighty-three to sixty-nine by seven-thirty. I thought I would freeze to death. I wrapped my chenille housecoat tight around me and pulled on a pair of ugly wool socks. Dottie, over at the nursing home knitted the socks for me. She started out one year crocheting a pair of slippers made from leftover yarn. They looked so awful that it took me two years before I could bear to put them on my feet. Then, I discovered how comfortable they were. I passed that information on to Dottie, who wondered why it took me two years to tell her, and she's been supplying me with slippers and socks ever since. They are still ugly. Which reminded me that she had another pair ready so I should pop in sometime today and pick them up. Dottie loves reading those mystery/romance novels so it's sort of an exchange: she gets rid of all her leftover yarn and I get rid of old second hand books that no one will buy.

As I descended the stairs, I yelled, "All right, every cat in this house must assemble at the back door. You have thirty minutes to do your business and explore the back yard before I leave for work."

I'm sure they understand because all seven of them race for the door. I open it and they scatter in seven different directions. Out of them all, Phyl is the only one that will return on time. Usually, I let the others run wild all morning. So far, I've had only about a dozen complaints, which isn't bad, considering. They seem to have an inner clock system though and as soon as I open the back door at noon, they all gather there, rush in, and head straight for the food dishes. After that, they sleep until I return home from work. And, they talk about a dog's life - dogs have nothing on those cats of mine.

I was actually busy all morning. Flori came in for coffee and this time, I'm happy to announce, she remembered her cinnamon buns.

"I'm sorry that they're not fresh, Mabel." She apologized for the umpteenth time. To Flori, if they're out of the oven for more than two hours, they are bordering on stale.

"They're wonderful. I think I like them better the next day. The brown sugar maple syrup has more time to soak through the dough." I explained as the syrup rolled down my chin. Flori makes the best cinnamon buns in the world. And, that's no exaggeration.

It was after eleven and the store was empty now. Beth Smee, Reg's wife, was in shortly after nine. I really like Beth and she reads more books than anyone else in Parson's Cove so I didn't want to put her on the spot. She did supply, voluntarily and unknowingly, some information on her own. Apparently, Reg was very hesitant about arresting Melanie but felt that with the evidence that he had, he had no choice.

"Really?" I said. "I knew Reg would never arrest anyone without sufficient evidence. What do you think, Beth? Do you think it was sufficient?"

Whether she thought I was trying to pry information or not, she never let on. She just said, "I have no idea, Mabel. You know I never get involved in his cases." With that, she started shuffling through a box of books.

However, before she went out the door, she said, "I think Reg said that the whole case is resting on the testimony of one person. Or, something like that."

Before she got outside, I ran to the door. "A witness? Who's the witness, Beth?"

She shrugged. "As I told you, Mabel, I never get involved. Most of the time, I'm not even listening to him." She smiled. "I know Reg appreciates all the help you give him but I think he said that this time he and the boys could solve it on their own." She patted my arm. "That I do remember hearing him saying." Another smile and she was gone.

I turned to Flori. "Flori, did you hear that? They have a witness."

"Mabel, all I heard was Beth saying that Reg and the boys could solve it on their own. Didn't you hear that part?"

"Of course, I did. Reg always says that. Weren't *you* listening? There's a witness. Do you think someone actually saw Melanie hitting Bernie over the head with a brick?"

Flori blushed and looked down at her empty coffee cup.

"You know something about it, don't you?" Flori is so easy to read. "What have you been keeping from me, my best friend?"

Her face turned a brighter shade of pink. "I'm really not keeping anything from you, Mabel. It's only what Jake heard at the café and I know you don't trust anything that Jake says."

"Okay, but I might trust what someone else told him. So, what did her hear? Who's this witness?"

"Oh, Mabel, you know I hate gossiping, especially about murder. And, how do we know it's even true? What if I tell you something and it's completely false, but you won't know that so you'll go running to this person and they'll get into trouble and then, you'll come back to me and I'll be in trouble. It will end up being a big mess."

"First of all, Flori, you love gossip. Besides, we don't know if the information is wrong. And, maybe, just maybe, I won't go to the person at all. Why are you jumping to conclusions like that?"

"First of all, Mabel, even if the information is wrong, you *will* go to the person. I haven't been your friend for sixty years and not know that. Even if you knew that not a word of it was true, you'd go."

"Why don't you let me be the judge of that? Now, who was the witness and what did this witness, witness?"

Flori sighed. "Jake said they were talking about it at the café. Apparently, Prunella Flowers says she saw Bernie and Melanie having a big argument outside their car at the carwash and when they saw her watching them from across the street, they disappeared to the back of the carwash."

"You mean behind the carwash? By the lake?"

Flori gave me a resigning look and sighed. "Well, you know what's behind the carwash – it's the lake."

"Prunella? The witness? I'm amazed she even came forward. Can we really trust her, Flori?"

"Can *we* trust her? We, as in you and me, do not have to worry about it at all. I'm sure if she saw Bernie and Melanie arguing, she saw what she saw. End of story, Mabel."

"But that doesn't prove that Melanie killed Bernie, does it? It just proves that they were arguing and were together behind the carwash."

"I have no idea. This is entirely up to the police. They know more about it than we do and I'm sure they have lots more information and clues."

"Actually, Flori, I wasn't asking for an answer. That was sort of a rhetorical question."

Flori stood up and took her cup and the empty cinnamon bun pan into the back room to rinse out. It was almost noon now and time for me to start for home too.

We went out the front door together but before I headed in the opposite direction, she grabbed my arm and said, "Please don't get involved, Mabel. Don't go to visit Prunella. Just once let's have a murder without the name Mabel and Flori being attached to it."

I laughed. "You, my friend, are getting carried away, as usual. If I have a few spare minutes after I feed the cats, I'll be going over to the nursing home to visit Dottie. She has some more socks for me. I promise you, I will not be spending my lunch hour with Prunella."

It's hard to describe the look of relief on Flori's face. It almost made me feel guilty that I planned to visit Prunella in the evening.

There was no way I could eat any lunch after gorging myself on three of Flori's buns but I did have to let the cats back in the house. Sure enough, they were all standing on the step, waiting for me. I let them in, filled their food dishes and water dishes and then I left for the nursing home with a bag of books for Dottie.

There's a large sign on the lawn that says Parson's Cove Restful Retirement Retreat. I guess someone wanted it to sound like a luxury resort of some sort but the name doesn't fool anyone. No one forced to live there, feels like they're in Cancun, Mexico. It was actually quite an attractive building when it was built over forty years ago but I guess with all the cutbacks and layoffs, there isn't enough money to keep it beautiful. Dottie says she counts her blessings because she has a place to sleep at night. Dottie is one of those people who succeed in seeing good in everything - sort of a very small wrinkled version of Flori.

Noon was a good time to visit with Dottie because everyone was finished eating by then. They have breakfast at seven, lunch at eleven and their dinner at four-thirty. Then, she told me, if you're still hungry, you could go into the small residents' kitchen and make yourself a sandwich before bed. It all sounded quite nice to me but she just screwed up her face when I said that. I guess it all depends on if you like stale bread with peanut butter before you go to sleep.

When I arrived she was already outside sitting in a wooden lawn chair, soaking in some sun. At least with the cooler temperature, a person could sit outside without burning to a crisp. There was a breeze and the scent of lilacs and the buzz of some very large bees filled the air. The lawn chairs at the Parson's Cove Retirement Retreat are wooden, heavy and huge. I'm not sure if that's so they won't blow away or because they don't want any of the residents throwing them at the staff. Dottie looked like a small dot in that chair.

Her face lit up when she saw me. "Mabel, you came for your socks." Then she spotted the bag in my hand. "And you brought some books for me." She stood up and clapped her hands. People who find out they've won the lottery couldn't look any happier than Dottie does when she sees a bag of books.

By this time, everyone who was sitting outside was staring at us. Some were smiling and waving; others, scowling and drooling. Mr. Dudley was yelling my name.

"Let's get to your room before old Dudley attacks me, Dottie," I said. She grinned and I held her arm as we walked to the front door. Sam Dudley had it in his head that visiting Dottie was my excuse to see him. This obsession started a few weeks back but seemed to be getting more intense. I really didn't want to complain to the management but if he got any more aggressive, I was thinking that I might have to.

It was cool, semi-dark and pleasant in Dottie's cubbyhole of a room. There was only enough space for a few personal items. What she did have, she had to guard with her life because a few of her inmates were kleptomaniacs.

"So, what's new, Dottie?" I asked after she'd pulled my newly knitted socks from under her mattress. They were shaped like a squash and were a mixture of orange, purple, green, and black. I would never hurt her feelings but I doubted that anyone would steal any of the socks or slippers that she made. I sat down on her only chair and she sat on the bed facing me.

"There's never anything much new here. We're supposed to make our monthly trip to the city tomorrow. Now, I hear they want us to go every week. I can't figure out why. The management is always complaining about not having any money for trips or anything. Doesn't make any sense to me."

"I haven't heard anything about it. Do you like going, Dottie?"

She shrugged. "Not so much anymore. It used to be fun when they'd let us loose in the Mall but now, they drive to some park, make us get out and sit and then we have to wait for the bus to come and pick us up again. If I want to sit outside and look at the trees, I can do that here."

"You're kidding, every week? Is Bill Williams still driving you?"

She shook her head. "Not anymore. Now, Calvin Koots drives us. I don't know who drives his taxi when he's with us. Have you seen anyone driving it, Mabel?"

"You know, I do remember someone driving it. He went past the store one morning and I wondered what he was doing in Calvin's taxi. You know who it was, Dottie?"

She shook her head. "I can't read your mind, Mabel."

"Sorry but now it makes me feel a little weird. It was Bernie."

Dottie's eyes popped open wide. "Bernie? I heard he was dead, Mabel. Murdered. Is that really true?"

"I'm afraid so. Reg locked up Melanie and charged her with his murder. Well, I imagine they'll call it manslaughter. They say she hit him on the head with a brick and then pushed him into the lake."

"Oh, I don't believe that for one minute, do you, Mabel?"

"Well, I do believe the brick and the lake but that's about all. I don't think Melanie would do it either but apparently Prunella saw them arguing just before Bernie was killed."

"Since when does that prove murder? My old man and I used to fight all the time. Good thing he died of natural causes or I might've been charged."

"Well, it sounds like Melanie would inherit a large sum of money from an insurance policy that Bernie took out just before he died."

"That's all circumstantial. I've read enough books to know that."

I glanced at the clock on the nightstand. "Well, I'd better get moving. Have to open the shop in ten minutes."

Dottie turned the plastic bag upside down and dumped the books on the bed. "Let me know how the murder investigation goes," she said, but before I could say anything except goodbye, she was already beginning to read.

Flori stopped in about three. The cooler temperature did wonders for her hair and personality. She was fairly bubbling when she walked in. Her hair was bright, shiny and back to its slick new style. She'd applied fresh makeup. Her lips were a soft coral and her artificially arched eyebrows, a dark auburn.

"Hmmm, Flori," I said. "You're looking as good as you smell this afternoon. Is that a new outfit?"

She was wearing a light turquoise and coral flowered dress that came down almost to her ankles. It had an empire waist with a very modest neckline. Hot pink earrings dangled all the way down to her shoulders. It's true she was wearing flip-flops on her feet but they were such a dark turquoise that you hardly noticed that they were plastic.

"I'm so happy this dreadful heat has come to an end that I felt like celebrating. We can even have a cup of coffee without that loud old air conditioner on."

"That's true, and guess what? I have a fresh pot on."

"I'm sorry I didn't bring anything over to eat with it, Mabel."

"Are you kidding? I can still taste those wonderful cinnamon buns that I ate this morning."

"You mean you haven't eaten anything since then?" She jumped up off the chair. "I'm going home right now and make some ham and cheese sandwiches for you."

I grabbed the full cup of coffee from her hand and gently pushed her back down.

"No, you're not. We're going to sit and have a visit." I fixed my coffee and pulled a chair over to be closer. "I was talking to Dottie at noon and she tells me that the seniors' home is now taking them into the city every week."

Flori stared at me over her cup. "Really? That's lovely, isn't it? I'm sure they appreciate it. I wish I could go with them. I never get to shop over there. You know this new outfit, Mabel? It came from the city but my daughter bought it for me." She sighed. "I don't know why those girls of mine never ask me to go with them." Tears welled up in her eyes. "It really hurts sometimes. Did you know that?"

"I know it hurts. But some of it is your own fault. Why do you always insist that they take me too? They don't want me hanging around with them. You have to go without me, Flori."

"The thing is, Mabel, you need clothes worse than I do. It would be nothing for you to get Delores to come in some afternoon and we could go shopping."

I looked down at my neatly pressed jeans and white cotton shirt. Compared to Flori, I looked quite drab. On the other hand, almost everyone looked drab beside Flori. She was scrutinizing me, too.

"You could use some color. Why do you always insist on wearing non-colors, Mabel?"

"Non-colors? My jeans are blue. That's a color."

Flori rolled her eyes. "I have an idea. Why don't we see if we can go with the folks from the seniors' home? You know, we could be like chaperones."

"They don't go shopping."

"What do you mean? They always go shopping. The bus drops them off at the mall and they shop till they drop."

I shook my head. "Not any more. Dottie says that now they drive to some park, drop them all off, and then come back later to get them and take them home."

"But I know that's not what they're supposed to do, Mabel. I was at the town council meeting when they talked about that. They arranged for the school bus to take them to the city once a month for shopping. Bill Williams, the school bus driver, was getting paid extra to do that."

"Well," I said, draining my cup, "that's not what's happening. You should check it out, Flori."

"You know I will. Jake can have a talk with Bill and see what he's up to."

"It's not Bill who's driving them. It's Calvin Koots."

"Calvin? Well, who's driving his taxi while he's gallivanting off to the city?"

"Bernie Bernstein."

"Really? But Bernie's dead."

"As I said, Flori, you'd better check it out."

Chapter Eight

Prunella Flowers was sitting on her front porch nursing a glass of something she was trying to make everyone believe was iced tea but believe you me - that was no glass of iced tea. I know the aroma of rum when I smell it. Personally, I enjoy a nip of gin once in awhile. Flori is horrified that I do. She'll imbibe in wine. When I say 'imbibe', I'm talking about one of the rarer meanings of the word and that is, absorb. To her, wine is Biblical but gin is a sin.

Before Prunella could protest, I walked up onto the porch and sat down.

"Oh Mabel, I don't know if I'm up to visiting with anyone tonight. It's nice to see you but as you probably know, I've had the police here so many times today and I've had to go down to the station to make a statement. I don't want to hurt your feelings but I think I just want to sit here and drink my iced tea and try to relax." As she spoke, her arms fluttered and some of her rum slopped over the side of the glass. When she saw what happened, she quickly put the glass to her lips and licked the 'iced tea' before it dripped on her shirt.

I reached over and patted her arm. "I don't blame you one bit, Prunella. If I were you, I wouldn't be drinking iced tea; I'd be drinking something a lot stronger. It must be terrifying for you. Imagine seeing Melanie only minutes before she smashed her husband on the head and sent him into another world."

(Not that I believe in another world but I was trying to make it sound as dramatic as I could.)

"Oh Mabel, if I'd known what was about to happen, I would've called Reg right away." Her thin arms began to shake and she was having some trouble hanging onto that iced tea.

"Prunella, why don't we go inside and I'll make you a better drink. Do you happen to have any rum in the house?"

She almost fell over when she stood up but I grabbed her in time and helped her into the kitchen.

When we got inside, she said, "I think I might have some rum, Mabel. Would you like a little drink too? I hate to drink alone."

"Of course, I'll join you. Where is the bottle?" I steered her into one of the kitchen chairs and sat her down.

Her face turned pink and she pointed to the counter with one fluttery finger. "Well, I think it's right over there on the cupboard."

Sure enough, there was the half-full (or half-empty, whichever way you look at it), bottle of dark golden rum sitting right on the kitchen counter. Imagine that.

"Do you want me to pour out your iced tea?" I asked, very innocently.

She blushed. "Well, if you must know, Mabel, it really isn't iced tea. I know you must think I'm terrible but I poured myself some rum and cola."

"I don't think you're terrible at all. You are very shaky, Prunella. Have you eaten anything lately? Did you have some dinner?"

She shook her head. "I can't eat anything. This murder thing has messed up my life, Mabel. What am I going to do? My stomach is churning all the time. Reg says that I might have to go to court and testify. What if I didn't hear right? What if I made a mistake and Melanie goes to jail for life because of me? Or worse yet, what if she gets the death penalty?" With that thought in mind, she put her head in her arms on the table and sobbed. It wasn't the loud wet sort of sobbing that Flori does but it was a quiet moaning sort of sobbing. I sat there for a few minutes and patted her back.

"Prunella," I said. "What exactly did you hear Melanie saying to Bernie? And, don't worry, we don't have the death penalty here. This isn't Texas, you know."

It seemed that she suddenly woke up to reality. She sat up and reached for a tissue from a box on the table.

"Oh Mabel, I'm sorry I broke down like that." She blew her nose and kept the tissues rolled up in her fist. Then she turned to me and said in a very quiet serious voice, "I'm sorry, Mabel, but Sheriff Smee specifically said that I should not tell anyone and especially you, what I heard that morning."

"Really? Why did Reg say that? He knows very well that a woman has to confide in another woman. That's the problem with having a male sheriff, Prunella. They don't understand anything when it comes to dealing with women. Now, if you asked his wife Beth if you should talk about what happened with your friends, she would know exactly what you should do – you should talk it out. If you did that, you wouldn't be sitting on the porch all day drinking rum. I've a mind to talk to Reg and tell him what he's doing to you."

She grabbed my arm. "Oh no, Mabel, please don't tell Reg that I've been drinking." After clearing her throat, she continued, "I did have a problem with alcohol at one point in my life. Do you really think it would help if I talked about it? The murder, that is."

"You know that it would. It's a heavy burden for one person to bear and you shouldn't have to. Reg knows very well that I've helped him solve a number of murder cases so I don't know why he's being so stubborn with this one."

Prunella took a gulp of the rum and cola. "I know why," she said. "I think he might be jealous, Mabel. And, he's retiring so maybe he wants to leave some sort of legacy. That's what men are like, aren't they?" She grinned as if she and I were sharing some undiscovered secret.

I grinned back. "I'll make myself that drink now."

In the fridge, I found some cold cuts and cheese so I took those out, along with a canned soda and a jar of dill pickles. There were some almost fresh buns in a bag on the counter so I took one out and made a sandwich for her. Prunella sat, looking very gloomy and every now and then taking a sip of her drink. I wanted her to eat before she passed out on me.

I plunked the sandwich down on a plate and put it in front of her.

"Here, eat. I'll freshen up your drink." I emptied the glass and poured in a small amount of rum with a large amount of cola. In my glass, I did the same – except the opposite. After all, I hadn't been drinking all day.

While she ate, I talked about everything that was happening in Parson's Cove except the murder. There wasn't much to talk about but I wanted her to relax. I told her about the senior citizens going into the city every week now and how they couldn't even go shopping anymore. She thought that was terrible too. Someday, I told her, she and I should go with them and force Calvin Koots to drop all of us at the Mall.

"And," she said, quite excitedly, "we'd tell him that we would watch over them. How could he say no to that?"

I didn't want to tell her that I wasn't too fussy about babysitting a bunch of golden oldies, especially old Mr.

Dudley, but I was happy that she was settling down and had stopped being so fluttery.

She was finished her sandwich so I asked if she would like some coffee.

"Oh yes, that would be so wonderful. I'm told that you make the best coffee in Parson's Cove."

"You mean in all these years, you've never stopped in at the shop and had a cup of my coffee?"

"I've been in your shop, you know that, but I've never had a cup of coffee there."

I knew Prunella stopped in once in awhile but I also knew that she never bought anything so I never offered her coffee. If I started giving coffee to everyone, the place would be full every day but not with customers. Sometimes I see Prunella walking around with Esther Flynn and I obviously never offer coffee to Esther.

"Well, you're in for a treat, Prunella." It wasn't hard to find everything so in a matter of minutes, there was a pot of coffee brewing.

Prunella pushed her rum away. It was still full. I placed the coffee in front of her and took the glass away. I'm sure she realized that she'd reached her limit in the rum department.

"So, Prunella," I said. "What exactly bothers you so much about what you heard? Is it that you're not sure now what Melanie said?" She hesitated as though she wasn't sure if she should answer. "You don't have to tell me what she said. I know Reg told you not to and I don't want to get you in trouble but I think you should tell me why you're so upset or worried about it. I know it would make you feel better."

She took a drink of coffee and savored it for a few seconds before swallowing. "This is wonderful coffee, Mabel." She smiled and thanked me. "In fact, you're nothing like Esther makes you out to be."

It was my turn to smile. "I know."

She laughed. "Oh no, I know what I heard. I guess that is what's bothering me the most, Mabel." She looked at me with a sad smile. "It's hard because I was married for over forty years before my husband passed away and never in all those years did I raise my voice to him and tell him that I hated him and wanted him to go to hell." She shook her head. "Even when I was angry with him, I never would've told him that I was going to kill him."

"Melanie told Bernie that she was going to kill him?"

She nodded. "That's why I went to the police. Do you think I did the right thing?"

"Yes, you did. If she did kill him in a moment of heated passion, I'm sure they'll call it manslaughter. It definitely wasn't something that she planned ahead of time."

"They called each other a lot of terrible names, Mabel. I wouldn't even repeat them. Except Reg made me tell him, but I told him that I would say them only once and never again. That's why I had to go to the station so they could make a video. It was so humiliating."

"It's something that they have to do, Prunella. You were very brave to say all those words."

I looked at my watch. It was after nine. By now, Flori would've called my house about five or six times and maybe she would be sitting on my back step waiting for me.

"I guess I'd better get home, Prunella. Are you going to be okay now? There's still some coffee left if you want another cup. It might keep you up all night though."

Prunella stood up, much more steady than the last time. "I think I might leave it and warm it up in the morning. That should wake me up good." She walked me to the door. "I want to thank you so much for coming over, Mabel. You're the only person who has. Esther hasn't even come and she's supposed to be my friend. I was feeling so lonely and wondering if everyone in Parson's Cove had abandoned me."

Although I'm not the hugging type of person, I stepped over and gave her a hug. I didn't think she was ever going to let me go.

Flori was sitting on my back step when I got home.

Chapter Nine

"Flori," I said. "What on earth are you doing here?"

"You know very well what I'm doing here." She stood up. Considering the fact that she is already almost a foot taller than I am and then add my back steps to that, I felt like an ant preparing to be squished.

"Well, my goodness." I smiled. "Don't just stand there. Come on in." I tried to maneuver around her as nonchalantly as I could but she wasn't going to let me get away with it that easily.

"No, Mabel, I'm not coming in. I've been waiting here for almost an hour. I phoned three times before I came. Where, on earth have you been? And, don't tell me you were working at the store because I already called there and there was no answer."

"I had some errands to run, that's all. You didn't have to worry about me, Flori. Why do you want to stay outside on the step? You can come in and I'll make us a cup of tea."

"What kind of errands do you have to run in the evening, Mabel?" She crossed her arms. This is no easy feat for her as her breasts tend to get in the way. So, there she stood, trying to stare me down and trying to keep her arms together. "Did they happen to involve Prunella?"

"Did what involve Prunella?"

"Your errands, Mabel."

I know Flori well enough to know that she already knew I'd been at Prunella's house. There was no point in prolonging the pain.

"As a matter of fact, it did if you must know."

She dropped her arms down. "It's a good thing you came clean because I had proof that you were there."

"You had proof?"

"Hmm-hmm. It just so happens that Jake saw you sitting on the veranda with Prunella. And, you thought I wouldn't find out about your investigating, didn't you?"

"Flori, I have absolutely nothing to hide. I'm so thankful that I was able to visit with her. Do you know that the whole town is avoiding her and she's suffering from depression because of it?"

Flori's cheeks turned a tiny bit pink because her conscience always bothers her if someone is in need and there's no one there to help. She feels like all the problems in Parson's Cove are resting upon her shoulders.

Her arms dropped and a look of horror crossed her face. "Oh, Mabel, I had no idea. You know that I would've gone over to visit if I'd known. What's going to happen to her?"

"Hopefully, nothing, but I can tell you if she doesn't stop drinking all those large glasses of iced tea, she'll be in bad shape soon."

"Iced tea? Why would that hurt her?"

"It does if she's saying it's iced tea and really it's rum and coke."

Flori gasped. "Oh my goodness, Mabel, does Reg know? If she's been drinking, they won't be able to use her testimony, will they? Do you think she was drunk when she thought she saw Melanie and Bernie fighting?"

I grabbed her arm and turned her towards the door. "Flori, come in. We can't talk about this outside. Besides, who knows who's hiding behind the bushes listening?"

I opened the door but not before Flori quickly glanced around my back yard.

"I have lots to tell you, Flori, so I'm going to dig out a bottle of Sadie MacIntosh's wine. Why don't you sit in the living room? I'll get the wine and some snacks."

"What do you mean - you have lots to tell me? You aren't thinking of trying to solve a mystery here, are you? You said that Prunella wasn't drunk so, Mabel, she saw what she saw. Please don't try to read things into it. Please leave it up to Reg and the boys. Please don't include me in anything."

"Flori, go and sit down. If you say 'please' once more, I'll scream."

I heard Flori sigh or perhaps it was more of a groan before she plunked down on the couch. Several springs protested because it isn't often that someone that size tests their integrity. It seemed that even though the couch was over fifty years old, it has stood the test of time and Flori was not in any danger of having a sharp spring fly up anywhere into her anatomy. I'm always a bit leery when she sits on any of my furniture. I know if something ever breaks, she will be heartbroken. It will do damage to her self-esteem that could never be repaired.

My pantry, which used to be my father's bedroom, is off the kitchen. It holds a small freezer,
(which I try to keep filled with my homemade muffins) four large plastic kitty litter boxes, seven cat dishes, and three large dishes for water (which all say DOG on them). Along the north wall, there are three shelves filled with small appliances, mixing bowls, and other items that I don't use too often. On the south wall, there is a large antique hutch - where in the bottom cupboard, I store my wine supply. Sadie makes the best chokecherry wine in the country. I'm sure it's fifty

percent alcohol. The one window faces east. I'm proud to say that this is the largest pantry in Parson's Cove.

Instead of pouring the wine I just grabbed two wine glasses, the bottle, and a corkscrew and went into the living room.

"I thought you were going to bring some snacks." Flori doesn't miss a thing.

"I will. I can't carry everything at the same time, Flori."

Flori jumped up. "Oh Mabel, I'm so sorry. What was I thinking? I'll go and bring the snacks."

"No, you won't. I'll bring the snacks while you open the wine and pour it." I handed the corkscrew to her. "And don't be stingy with the wine."

I never have much for snacks in my house but I did have some excellent old cheddar cheese, an almost empty box of Ritz crackers, and three dill pickles. After cutting up the cheese and pickles and arranging the crackers around the outside of the plate, it looked like something a person could take to a baby shower. Speaking from experience, of course, since Flori's daughters or daughters - in - law seem to be having a baby every year or so and this is what I always bring.

Flori, I am happy to say, was not stingy with the wine. In fact, she was half way through her first glass when I walked in with the snacks.

"Flori," I said. "You do not guzzle wine. Beer, you guzzle. Wine, you sip." I placed the plate on the table in front of her. "Sorry but this is all I have. I can thaw out some muffins if you like but somehow they don't go with wine, do they?"

She took another gulp. A few drops dribbled down her chin. She expertly guided them back into her mouth with her finger.

"I didn't come to eat so don't worry about it, Mabel." She picked up three chunks of cheese and four crackers. "I think we might need some napkins though."

After getting Flori settled in, I took my first swallow. Sadie's wine has as much alcohol in it as most tequila does and probably twice that of Prunella's rum. I think it was the first time all evening that I started to relax.

"So, Mabel, what's the news you had to tell me? You said you had plenty."

I leaned back in the couch and munched on a piece of cheese.

"Well, let's see. Melanie and Bernie obviously had a huge fight. Prunella said they were swearing at each other."

"That's it?" She drained the glass and refilled it.

"Well, I guess it was bad enough that Reg thought she was guilty of murder."

Flori held her glass up as if admiring the red glow – a glow that was beginning to spread up to her face. She swirled the wine and then finished it off in one swig.

"That's it, Flori, you are finished drinking wine for tonight. You're worse than Prunella. You better eat the pickles now so you can walk home, sober."

"Oh for Pete's sake, you know I can hold my liquor. By the way, I don't think anyone can be charged with murder for just arguing with your mate."

"But I guess you can if you're telling him that you're going to kill him."

Flori's eyes popped. "She said she was going to kill him?"

I nodded.

"I guess that does make a difference." She finished off the rest of the cheese, crackers and pickles in silence.

Chapter Ten

My next task was going to be much harder than trying to get Prunella to talk. Someway, somehow, I had to get in to visit Melanie in jail. Not that it's a real jail. There's a tiny windowless room at the police station and in it, Reg stashes his worst criminals. The door does look jail-like, however, as it has a small square window in it and the lock is on the outside. There's barely enough room for one person to turn around but there are two small cots and I know that one time Reg did keep two nasty prisoners in there for a day or so. Mostly, Amos is in there sleeping off a drinking binge. I think Reg puts him there for Amos' own protection.

Opportunity knocked the next day just before noon. I happened to look out my shop window and saw Reg driving home for lunch. There was no time for procrastinating. I quickly swung my 'Closed' sign up and locked the door. Mutt, who has his hardware store next to me, saw me walking past but I didn't make eye contact. His door opened and he yelled my name but I didn't miss a step. It's easier when you're older and can pretend you're hard of hearing.

I was walking up to the station door before it struck me that I'd still have to get past the two deputies. If only Scully was there, I might have a fighting chance. There wasn't much hope getting past both of them.

I slowly opened the door. The reception area was empty. However, there were voices coming from Reg's office. I slipped into the room, gently closed the door behind me and listened. It was Scully and Jim and as far as I could make out they were fighting over who was going to sit in Reg's big leather chair. I figured that ought to give me enough time to sneak into the back room.

There's a short hallway off the reception area. On one side is the cell and on the other there are two rooms: a restroom and a coffee room. Reg had locked the cell door but the key was in the lock so I turned it and went in.

Melanie was lying curled up on one of the cots in a fetal position. The only light came from the hallway so I couldn't see too well; however, even in the semi-darkness I knew that her whole face was swollen from crying. It looked as if her hair hadn't seen a comb or brush in days and it was easy to see she'd been sleeping in her clothes.

I quickly walked over to her and put my finger to my lips. One scream from her and I would've been out on my ear. She stared at me and slowly nodded her head.

"Are you going to be all right?" I whispered.

She shook her head. "I killed my husband," she whispered. "I killed Bernie."

"Are you sure you did?" I asked. "Can you tell me what happened, Melanie? I'm going to try to help you."

For one brief moment I saw a glimpse up hope in her eyes but it faded quickly.

"I don't think you can, Mabel. I've already confessed."

"You confessed? Why did you confess?"

"Because I killed him, that's why."

"Melanie, tell me exactly what happened, okay? Don't leave anything out."

"We were at the carwash. Bernie had this thing lately about keeping the car so clean." She stopped. "I don't know why that bothered me so much. It seems so stupid now. It was like he was fanatical. He was washing his car every second day. It was driving me crazy. We were on our way to Mom and Dad's and suddenly he pulled into the carwash again. He jumped out to make change and I jumped out after him. I know it isn't much but it's five dollars every time and we don't have that much money to waste. I guess I just lost it, Mabel. We were going to be late for dinner at my parent's house and there he was, trying to get change to wash the stupid car. I followed him to that little box at the side of the building and I guess I was screaming really loud but he didn't pay any attention to me. I told him that I wished he were dead. He started yelling at me then. I can't remember everything that we said. It must've sounded terrible. When he said he didn't want me in his life anymore, I hit him."

"With the brick?"

"No, not with a brick. With my fist. That's when I saw Prunella standing across the street and staring. I was so mad at Bernie for letting people see us fight that I pushed him out to the back of the washing bay. He started hitting me back then. I gave him a hard push and he stumbled. He went down on one knee and I picked something up and threw it at him. Then, I saw him stumble backwards over a rock sticking out of the sand and he fell into the water."

"You picked up a brick?"

She put her hands over her face for a moment and then looked up at me. "I didn't think it was a brick. I thought it was a stone but they tell me that it was a brick."

"Who's 'they?'"

"Well, almost everyone. That's what killed Bernie and since I'm the one who fought with him and threw something at him, it had to be me, didn't it?"

"No, it didn't have to be you. Someone could've come after you left. Didn't you think of that?"

"Yeah, but who? Who would want to kill Bernie besides me?"

"I don't know but I think we should try to find out. Why did you sit in the car so long waiting for him to come back?"

"That's another thing they have against me. It looks like I killed him and then waited before calling Reg."

"So, why didn't you go to check on him sooner? Why did you wait so long?"

"Oh, Mabel, I don't know. I was so mad at him and the longer he took coming back, the madder I got. Mommy called me on my cell phone and I told her that Bernie was working and we wouldn't be able to make it for supper."

"Another lie. You weren't doing yourself any favors, were you? So, what did you do for those two hours anyway?"

"It was so hot, I let the car run and turned the air on. I figured Bernie could sweat outside but I'd keep nice and cool. I dozed off. Well, that is until Esther woke me up."

"Esther woke you up?"

She nodded. "She banged on the window. She said she thought I had passed out from carbon monoxide poisoning."

"Oh brother, she didn't realize that there's plenty of air circulating through an open carwash bay? How dumb can a person be?"

"That's when I went to look for Bernie. At first, I thought he was so mad that he just left me and went home. I wouldn't have blamed him. I went out the back and there he was. Dead."

"And nosey Esther Flynn followed you?"

"Yes. I wish it would've been anyone else but her. She went all hysterical which didn't help because I was already hysterical."

"Can you remember what you said to her, Melanie? Did you give her any reason to think that it might've been your fault?"

At this, she started to cry. In between her sobs, she said, "I thought I'd killed him, Mabel. There was blood on his head and I didn't remember seeing it when I hit him before but there was no one else."

"In other words, you told Esther that you'd killed your husband?"

She looked at me with wide empty eyes. "I did."

"And, Esther went to Sheriff Smee?"

She nodded.

"Did he believe Esther?"

"At first, I don't think he did. He brought me in for questioning but was sure that it had been an accident or something. Then, Prunella came in and told him how she'd seen us arguing. I think Esther told her that she had to. Reg still didn't think I could be guilty because I told him that I just picked up a rock and threw it at Bernie. I was sure it was a rock. Not even a very big one. That stone couldn't have killed anyone, Mabel."

"Who discovered the brick?"

She sniffed and blew her nose. "One of the boys found it in the bush. Jim, I think."

I'd been so engrossed in Melanie's testimony that I momentarily forgot where I was. Suddenly, from the front room, I could hear Reg's booming voice.

"Melanie," I said. "I have to get out of here fast. If I manage to escape, don't tell Reg I was here, okay?"

"I won't."

"I'm going to find out who really killed Bernie. Don't give up now."

I walked to the door and peeked out. It looked like reception area was empty but I didn't dare try to escape out the front door. My only hope was the back. Before I could reach it, however, I heard Reg coming my way, yelling, "And I don't want either one of you sitting in my chair, got that?"

I quickly jumped across the hallway, popped into the washroom and shut the door. The light was off and I couldn't see a thing so I moved along the wall. If Reg opened the door, I would be behind it. If any of them came in to use the facilities, I would be as dead as Bernie was.

A moment later, there was another bellow.

"Which one of you boys left this door open and unlocked? How many times do I have to tell you that this is a jail cell and it must be kept locked when we have someone in it who has actually committed a crime? Well, which one of you left it open?"

There was silence and then Scully said, "It was locked."

I heard Reg walk into the room and say, "Melanie, are you all right?" Whatever she said, I didn't hear but obviously she didn't mention my name because next he asked, "Did you happen to have any visitors while I was away? Someone who came in and left without closing the door?"

My heart was pounding in my ears so hard I thought my head would explode.

Melanie must be an excellent liar because the next thing I heard was Reg telling Scully to run over to the Main Street Café and bring some lunch for the prisoner.

"I'm going to leave the door open for you, Melanie, so you can get some air in that cell. If you need anything, you just give a shout. I'm going to be in the office doing some paper work."

So much for making sure everyone kept the door locked in case the murderer might escape.

All three left for the front of the building. I gave Melanie the thumbs up before I snuck out the back door.

Chapter Eleven

Flori came into the store the next morning with a loud announcement. I had planned to spend my lunch hour at the crime scene but I didn't dare tell her that. When she insisted on bringing some of her homemade soup over, what could I say? She would know something was wrong if I rejected her offer.

"And, not only that, Mabel," she said. "I booked a place for us on the seniors' bus for Friday."

"You what?"

"I booked a place for us on the seniors' bus for Friday."

"I know what you said; I just don't know why you did it."

Right away, I could see that I'd hurt her feelings.

"But, Mabel, weren't you the one who suggested it? You were the one who said it wasn't fair. You can't back out now. Dottie is so excited that you're coming."

"You talked to Dottie about it?"

Flori's eyes started welling up. "I thought you would be happy, Mabel. I'm sure we discussed it. Remember, you were so upset because they dump everyone in that park and don't let them go shopping? Remember?"

I walked over and patted Flori on the shoulder. "Of course, I remember. It is upsetting. I didn't realize you were all that concerned too."

"How can you say that, Mabel? You know I love those old people as much as you do. I talked to Jake about it and he called the Retirement Home. They're so happy about us going with them. They have a new manager there. Sam Kinney. Jake asked him if we could accompany them every week and he said he'd consider it. I think we could do it, don't you? I'm sure Delores would love to come and watch the shop for you. Or, better yet, you could put a sign in the window to let everyone know you would be closed Fridays so you could help out the seniors. The townspeople would be so impressed. I'm sure your business would improve. What do you think, Mabel?"

"First of all, Flori, I would *never* consider going on that bus every week. Secondly, I would not even for one second consider putting a sign up saying that I was helping out old people and thirdly, Flori, you know very well I couldn't care less what the so-called townspeople think."

Tears were forming quickly in Flori's eyes.

"However, Flori, I will agree to go this Friday with you."

"Oh thank you. I knew you would." She proceeded to get up off the chair and crush me almost to death. When she reached the door, she turned and said, "And I've booked us for the next Friday as well." With that, she opened the door and disappeared from sight.

I'd been had.

There was one positive side to Flori's rushing out the door before I could throw something at her (which I would never do) – I could now visit the crime scene and not have to worry about any interference.

At five minutes before twelve, I locked the front door, hung up my closed sign and left out the back door. The back lane looked clear all the way to the carwash. I would have to get across one intersection, however, and that could be tricky. It was a slow day in Parson's Cove so there was a good chance I could get across without anybody spotting me.

Charlie Thompson's little house is not far from the carwash. After Charlie's place, there's a narrow empty lot and then Murray McFerguson's house. Murray must have about an acre because there are no more houses after his place. The McFerguson's stick to themselves but you do see Murray walking around town with his dog quite often. This reminded me that someone had also murdered Biscuit. Could the old hound have attacked whoever was in the process of murdering Bernie and got clobbered himself? Melanie never even mentioned the dog. I wished she'd never made that stupid confession.

When I reached the intersection, there was one car puttering down the street. I say puttering because it was Adolf Klassen. He's almost blind and as deaf as a rock but since he only drives from his house to the post office, no one complains. In fact, if Reg took his license away, probably half the town would be outraged. I say he'll keep driving until he runs over someone or something and then everyone will blame Reg. Once in awhile I do feel sorry for the sheriff.

Since Klassen is blind and I could walk faster than he could drive, I crossed the street. When I reached the other side, I heard him yell, "Watch where you're walking, mister. I almost ran over you."

I pretended I didn't hear and hurried down the lane to the carwash.

Sheriff Smee and his deputies had left a few signs to say that they'd been there. There were strips of yellow tape still clinging to some trees and there was a Styrofoam coffee cup sitting on a rock.

I stood back and surveyed the scene. The sand by the beach looked like a dozen people had trampled on it. You'd have to be an old Indian scout to read footprints in the sand anyway. I really had no idea what I was looking for. I guess anything to prove Melanie did not kill her husband. Anything to give reasonable doubt. Even that would please me.

Stupid Esther Flynn. Why didn't she stop to reason with Melanie before jumping to conclusions? Why did she make Prunella go to the police? If Melanie had to spend the rest of her days in prison, it would be stupid Esther Flynn's fault and I would go to any length to make her life as miserable as I could. I made that vow as I stood looking at the spot where Bernie Bernstein was murdered.

It only took a few seconds to make it so when I finished I decided to walk up to the carwash bay where Melanie had sat for two hours, waiting to see if her husband would return. Did Reg check to see if anyone else was getting their car washed at the same time? Maybe a witness saw someone else walking on the beach. Someone who could easily have come up after Melanie threw her little rock and that person could've hit him with the brick and killed him. I stood in the bay for a few minutes. It wasn't a drive-through bay because on the other side of the carwash, several feet away, was the lake. You drove in, washed your car and backed out. This is Parson's Cove so nothing is fancy like in the city. The water was pumped up from the lake and I'm sure the dirty water went right back in, although it wasn't supposed to - not with all those shampoos and phosphates. There were so many town meetings regarding pollution and contaminates before the carwash went in that I stopped going. They were going to do what they were going to do anyway.

I stood there thinking of Melanie sitting there for all that time with her husband lying dead not more than thirty or forty feet away. I went out the small door facing the water and walked down to the beach. There was no blood. There was nothing but the relaxing sound of water gently lapping up against the shore. I looked down the beach towards Charlie's house. Did he know something? One thing was certain - he would never go to the police. If he told anyone anything, it would be to me. He said there was some kind of mystery. Did it have anything to do with the murder?

I walked along the shore towards his place and McFerguson's. No one ever comes down to this part of the lake. The beach area is very narrow and you'd have to walk through private yards to get here. For sure no one would trespass through Charlie's yard. Not that he would harm anyone, he would probably sit and stare and that would make people very uncomfortable. As I walked, I watched the ground for any clues I could find. The Sheriff already had the murder weapon. I still can't understand Melanie not knowing if she picked up a stone or a brick. The murderer wasn't too bright if he left the murder weapon close by for someone to find. Not a professional hit man, in my opinion.

There was a high fence bordering Charlie's place. I remember when some of the men in town built that. Their wives were afraid Charlie might wander into the lake and drown. Like, he didn't have enough sense to walk around the fence and drown. As I said before, sometimes Charlie has more brainpower than most of them.

I stopped behind the McFerguson's house. There was a row of large old poplar trees bordering their lot. The house was quite a ways back. There was no movement at all. Poor Murray. Imagine having your dog killed by the same person who murdered your friend. I couldn't even grasp how I would feel if someone murdered Flori and then one of my cats.

A well-worn path went from their yard down to the beach. They had a boathouse sitting several feet out into the water and a boardwalk going out to it. There was an old aluminum fishing boat tied to a post and it bobbed up and down with each wave. I don't know how many times I saw Murray out in that boat with his dog hanging over the side, his head almost touching the water. That dog looked so sad but Murray insisted that he was the happiest dog in the world.

I hadn't learned anything visiting the crime scene but it did give me a better perspective. If it hadn't been so infernally hot out that day and Melanie hadn't had the a/c on, she probably would've heard Bernie fighting with someone. If she and Bernie hadn't been arguing, she would've gone to look for him after a few minutes. Perhaps, she would've made the change for the carwash herself.

I wondered if she was claiming guilt simply because she was feeling guilty about so many other things.

Chapter Twelve

Friday morning loomed before me. There was a dread in my heart as I looked out my bedroom window and saw the dull cloudy sky and the distant sound of thunder. After so many hot days, we knew this was coming but I was sincerely hoping it wouldn't come when I was with a busload of elderly people.

"No, this is good," Flori informed me when she called to make sure I was up. Really, she was making sure I hadn't skipped the country. "Now," she said, "we will have to go to the mall. That's what all the women want to do. Calvin has no excuse now. He can't dump us off at the park when it's raining."

I've known Calvin Koots all my life and trust me, he could drop us off at the park and disappear for hours if a hurricane was raging. I have never trusted that man. For years he drove an old taxi with Koots Taxi painted on the door and then last year he turned up one day with a brand new car. This one had Koots Taxi on the door too but Calvin didn't paint it with red barn paint. This one looked like a real taxi. Now, I ask you, how do you make enough money driving a taxi in Parson's Cove to afford a brand new fancy car like that? I have my own shop and I still drive my 1969 Buick. Mostly I see Calvin sitting in the Main Street Café drinking coffee and until last year, smoking. Now, at least, he has to sit outside to smoke.

After thinking of Calvin, I started thinking of Bernie. I'd seen the two of them together lately. Of course, in a small town it's hard to tell who is chummy with whom sometimes. We're sort of all stuck together whether we like it or not. Unless, it's Esther and me. The whole town would be in shock if they saw the two of us having coffee together at the café. But then, women are different than men; we know how to hold a grudge properly.

At nine on the dot Flori was at my door. It was out of her way and I'd told her that I'd meet her at the seniors' Home but she insisted we walk together. Delores was opening the store for me. I told her if it was a slow day, she could close up early. Knowing Delores she would have everything in the shop rearranged by noon. It's frustrating but she's cheap and she likes having a break from waiting on tables at Main Street Café.

By the time I'd grabbed my purse, the rain had started. By the time we got to the back step, it was coming down in torrents.

"I have a feeling they'll be cancelling the trip to the city," I said.

Flori shook her head. "Nope. Jake talked to Sam last night and he said Calvin insisted that they go even if it rains."

"Why would Calvin insist on such a thing? What's it to him if everyone goes or not?"

"I think it might have something to do with that new taxi, Mabel. Jake says he doesn't know how he can afford making payments with the little bit of money he makes."

"Oh well." I looked up at the blackening sky and the shot of lightning that seemed too close for comfort. "We'd better take my car. If we don't we'll get hit by lightning and then we'll never be able to take those ancient people to the city." For a moment that almost sounded like a solution to the problem. "Come on Flori, let's make a run for it."

Flori held up the umbrella but sharing an umbrella with her isn't what I would call sharing. By the time we reached the side door of my garage, water was running into my ear.

I drive a 1969 Buick Skylark. It's in pristine condition and every man, from sixteen to eighty-six, has offered to take if off my hands. Reg drools when I drive down the street. Personally, I don't see what the fuss is all about. I bought it secondhand in 1973 and it has never given me a hint of trouble. Why should I spend money on a new car when I don't have to?

We arrived at the Retirement Home before the bus did. Flori and I waited in the car by the front door. All we could see were noses pressed against the steamed-up glass. This certainly was an exciting day for them. All I could hope for was to die at home in my sleep and never have to live in that awful place.

"Flori," I said, "if anyone tries to put me in this place, take me out in that bush over there and shoot me."

"Don't talk like that. You know very well you'll be coming and living with me. I'll look after you." She reached over and grabbed my hand. There were tears in her eyes.

"When I'm ready to kick the bucket, how come you always think you're going to be so much healthier than me?" I squeezed her hand. "Not that I want to upset you, Flori, but you might even be gone before me."

"No, I won't. It's a known fact that married women live longer than single ones."

"That's not true, friend. Married *men* live longer than single men do but single *women* live longer than married women do. No, Flori, there's a good chance I'll live longer than you but, on the other hand I might be senile before you."

Fortunately, before Flori could burst into tears, the old school bus pulled up in front of us. Calvin opened the doors and I could see a cigarette flying through the air. At least, he flicked it out before everyone started boarding.

There was a slight letup in the rain. Obviously, the staff and residents noticed it too because the front doors flew open and suddenly everyone was making a mad dash for the bus.

Flori started to open the door but I stopped her. "Let all of them get in first, Flori. If we go now we'll just get trampled."

Also, I didn't want to tell Flori, but there was no way I was getting on that bus before Sam Lawson. I would board after he found his seat and then I would sit as far away as I could.

As it happened, Flori and I couldn't even sit together. Fortunately, Mr. Lawson sat at the back of the bus and since there was a seat right behind Mr. Koots, I sat there. I heard Sam yelling my name and then Flori calling and telling me that Mr. Lawson wanted to say hello but I kept looking straight ahead.

Mr. Kinney motioned to Calvin from inside the building. Calvin swore under his breath but got up and ran inside. I might've said a few choice words too if I'd had to run through that sheet of rain. I could see them talking and Calvin nodding but not looking too happy.

By the time Calvin got back inside the bus his shirt was soaking wet. He shoved the old bus into gear and away we went.

There was a lot of chatter going on. Flori's laughter filled the air. She was really enjoying this so I was glad that I'd come with her. I would rather be in Parson's Cove trying to solve a murder but then, how much can a person solve in a downpour? Besides, I wasn't sure what to do next.

Although I don't like Calvin, my heart isn't made of stone.

I reached over and touched his arm. "Calvin," I said, "sorry to hear about Bernie. I know you two were friends. It must've been quite a shock."

If I'd touched him with a branding iron, he couldn't have moved his arm faster.

"What do you mean, Mabel? Me and Bernie weren't friends. Where'd you get the idea we was?"

"Well, it's just that I saw the two of you having coffee together and one time I saw you in his truck. Seems I saw him driving your taxi too. That's all. I guess I took it for granted you were friends. I mean, Bernie and I were never friends but I'm shocked that someone would kill him."

At this, he turned and looked at me for a moment before turning back to his driving.

"I ain't saying it wasn't a shock. I'm saying we wasn't friends, that's all. And, why do you say *someone* killed him? You didn't know it was Melanie who did it?"

"Well, she says she did but I don't think it was her. She doesn't even remember picking up a brick. She thinks she picked up a stone and threw it at him. There's a big difference, you know. Personally, if I picked up a brick to hit someone on the head and it killed him, I would remember. Wouldn't you?"

Calvin shrugged. "I think it's something you shouldn't get involved in, Mabel. In other words, mind your own business."

"Why do you say that, Calvin?"

It seemed that Calvin suddenly became deaf. I repeated my question one decibel louder but he still didn't answer. Flori was sitting a couple of seats behind on the other side. I glanced back at her and she was giving me her evil eye. If Flori heard and probably half the bus, I'm sure the driver did too.

Mary Jane Smith was sitting beside me. She was close to a hundred and had taught school when I went. Her mind was as sharp as a tack but she was almost blind now and even with my loud voice, she turned to me and said, "My word, Mabel, you don't have to yell like that. Of course, Calvin knows it's going to be a wet day."

"You're right, Miss MJ." I guess everyone in town still calls her that. She didn't hear me but gave me a bright smile.

"I certainly hope Mr. Koots is not dropping us off in that awful park again. Did you bring your umbrella, Mabel?"

I nodded but then yelled "Yes" in her ear.

"Good for you. You were always one of my favorite pupils. I felt so bad about what Esther Flynn did to you. Have you ever forgiven her for that?"

I shook my head but then yelled "No" in her ear.

She broke out in a wicked grin. "Good for you. I would never forgive her either." It was quite exhilarating, sitting there giggling with my old English teacher.

I put my mouth right up to her ear and spoke very slowly but not loud enough for Calvin to hear. Of course, the way he was driving and changing gears, it probably didn't matter.

"Why don't you like going to the park?" I asked.

MJ insisted on speaking into my ear. "Because I think Koots is up to something."

I simply looked at her and raised my eyebrows. She pulled my head closer and went for the ear again.

"He leaves us alone for over two hours and when he comes back, he's always walking funny."

Into her ear: "What do mean, walking funny?"

Into my ear: "Like his feet are sore or something. I don't think he'd even get off his seat if we didn't insist that he help some of us onto the bus."

Into her ear: "Do you think he's been drinking?"

She shook her head and whispered, "No, I couldn't smell anything."

By this time, we were flying off the freeway. It seemed that Mr. Koots was in quite a hurry. The wipers were working overtime trying to keep the windshield clear. Every car and truck that drove by obliterated the view for several seconds.

From somewhere in the back of the bus, someone called out, "You're not taking us to that park again in this rain, are you?"

Again, Mr. Koots preferred to act deaf. Now, I could understand why Sam Kinney needed someone to travel with these people. The bus driver definitely had no senior skills. He could've been driving a truckload of cattle.

Flori spoke up. "No, Mrs. Kendal, Mr. Koots is taking us to the Bay Park Mall. Mr. Flanders had a talk with Mr. Kinney and you won't have to go to the park anymore unless you really want to."

A cheer went up. It seemed no one liked the park except our Mr. Koots.

I wondered why.

Chapter Thirteen

At least Calvin drove us to the front entrance instead of parking a mile away. Flori and I held our umbrella up for each person who got off the bus and walked them to the store. Of course, Mr. Lawson jumped the queue so I ended up holding the umbrella for him. I walked him as fast as I could without causing an accident and when I turned to help the next person, I felt a pat on my bottom.

"Mr. Lawson," I said. "If you ever touch me inappropriately again, you'll be walking home in the rain."

One of the women standing next to me said, "Good for you, Mabel. I told him the next time he did that to me, I was going to tell management and have him castrated."

I looked at the guilty party and said, "That's not an idle threat. I've already been responsible for four castrations so one more won't make any difference."

A silence fell over the group. The women smiled. The men looked everywhere but downwards. Old Man Lawson tried to laugh but it sounded more like a wheeze. Flori was speechless.

"Okay," I said. "Let's get organized. We're going to break up into groups of four. Everyone has to have a partner at all times. There's no way that Flori and I are going to run all over the mall hunting for someone when it's time to leave."

Flori took it from there.

"We will all meet back here right after lunch at 1:30. Does everyone understand?"

It was like letting the dogs out. I'm not sure if the 'four to a group' rule was followed or not. I did notice that none of them wandered off by themselves. Flori went out to check on Mr. Koots and to tell him where we would be waiting for him but Mr. Koots was gone.

I followed Flori around the stores. She's a much more enthusiastic shopper than I am. Mostly she looks for things for her kids or grandkids. Or, me. She gets so tired of seeing me in the same clothes all the time.

"You're getting to be just like Charlie Thompson," she tells me constantly.

"Well, Charlie and I like to be comfortable," I always tell her.

"Why don't you try a variety of colors, Mabel?"

"White and blue are colors," I say.

However, one store did get my attention.

"Hey, Flori," I said. "Let's check this store out."

Flori looked up at the sign.

"*SpyTown – Protect Your Spyware.* What kind of store is that?"

"I think it must sell all those little devices that detectives use to solve crimes, Flori."

"And why, pray tell, would you need anything like that?"

"I'm just curious, that's all. Aren't you?"

Flori shook her head. I'm not sure if it meant 'no' or it was done in frustration and bewilderment.

"I'll go and sit on the bench here, Mabel. You go and check out your little spy store."

I went in with great expectations and came out deflated. There was nothing there but computers and I imagine everything that goes with a computer. I didn't want to appear too dumb so when the vulgar young man behind the counter asked if I was having problems with spam, worms, or viruses, I politely told him that I'd never felt better in my life. Flori asked why I'd returned so quickly and I told her that everything was much too sophisticated for me. She smiled and said that she was glad I recognized my limitations.

"It takes a humble person to admit they can't be perfect in everything." She said this with a very smug look on her face.

Perhaps, it was time to advance to the next level and buy a computer. I mean, if I can handle a cordless phone with an attached answering machine, surely a computer can't be that much harder to figure out.

I knew Flori would be upset if I didn't purchase anything so when I found a store that carried animal toys, I bought something for each cat. I knew they would stand and look at it for a brief moment or two and then walk away, never to look again. However, it made Flori happy.

We had lunch in a cute little restaurant. Flori kept looking around for some of the old folks but it was as if they'd disappeared off the surface of the earth.

"I'm getting a little anxious," she said. "We haven't run into any of them. I hope they didn't get into any trouble. You know, maybe falling or something."

"Flori," I said after setting my cup down. "Trust me; those people can look after themselves. I'd be more worried about the people here, especially the store owners. Dolly says she has to hide everything because there are so many thieves in the seniors' home."

Flori looked out and watched the hoards of people aimlessly strolling from store to store. It was crowded because no one wanted to stay home on a miserable rainy day.

"I don't know. I still feel worried. If anyone gets into trouble we're the ones who will get hauled up on the carpet, you know."

"No, I'm the one who will be hauled up on the carpet, Flori."

"I hope all the men don't think you were serious about the castrating. Why, on earth, did you say you'd castrated four men? I couldn't believe you'd say such a terrible thing."

"I didn't say four *men*, I just said, 'four' and that I did - four of my cats."

"Oh, Mabel, that's hysterical." Flori giggled and the table shook. The man and woman in the next table looked over and started smiling too. In between her giggles, Flori told them, "Mabel castrated four." Tears started rolling down her cheeks. I handed her a handful of napkins. The man and woman got up and left.

I glanced at my watch. "Better dry up your tears and blow your nose, Flori, because it's almost time to meet Calvin." I stood up and grabbed the check. "This is my treat. You already spent your pension money for this month."

Flori grabbed up her five or six bags from under the table, I paid the bill, and off we went to find all the folks from the Retirement Home.

"I think," I said, "before we do anything else, we should check the food court. I'm sure that's where they would all eat."

The court was packed and it was noisy. There was one spot at the far end, however, that was far noisier than any other area. That's because almost everyone sitting there was deaf.

"There they are, Flori. I knew we'd find them here. Before we get too close and they spot us, let's count to see if we have them all."

I left that job up to Flori because I had no idea how many we started out with. As we walked up to them the women's faces lit up but for some reason the men didn't appear all that thrilled to see us. Well, most of them greeted Flori and of course, she ran around and gave everyone a big hug.

MJ got up and with the help of her cane, walked over to me. She leaned over and said into my ear, "Watch how Mr. Koots walks."

I nodded. I would've said more but the whole gang decided to rise up at the same time and suddenly we were propelling towards the front entrance of the mall. One good thing about leading a group of elderly, blind, deaf and drooling people is that everyone moves right out of your way. It didn't take long and we were all waiting at the entrance for our bus.

It was almost two before it pulled up in front of us. By this time everyone had to go to the washroom again so now Koots had to wait. I didn't feel sorry for him one bit. When MJ returned, she came up close to me and said, "Make him get out and walk."

The rain had stopped but the sky was still heavy with dark clouds and any minute I knew there would be a cloudburst. I ran up to the door and waited for Calvin to open it.

"Calvin, would you please come out and help these folks carry their parcels into the bus."

"Why should I? I'm the driver here, not the butler."

"Listen," I said and put my hands on my hips. "Your job here is just hanging by a thread as it is. All I have to do is tell Jake that you were uncooperative and you won't be driving into the city anymore."

If looks could kill…

He pulled himself off the seat as if I was forcing him to change a Depends and slowly, like an old man himself, descended to the ground. I looked over at MJ and she was staring at him with a tiny smile on her lips.

We both watched carefully as Calvin begrudgingly carried one bag after another and put them in the bus. My old English teacher was right. Calvin wasn't walking normally. What did he have - pebbles in his shoes?

Chapter Fourteen

Flori burst into my shop the next morning. The rain had run its course and the sun was shining. The temperature was moderate and the high was going to be about seventy-three so everyone was smiling. Except for Flori.

"Have you heard the latest, Mabel?" She was dressed in a lovely yellow, orange, green pantsuit with a matching green headband. The top was all flowery and the pants were solid green. Her sleek light auburn hair shone in the sunlight. Her artistically made up eyebrows arched up under her bangs. Obviously, her appearance didn't match her mood.

"I hope by the look on your face that there's been no more murders or accidents or anything negative at all. What's the matter?"

"It's Bernie." She burst into tears. I steered her over to the chair and handed her the box of tissues.

"What do you mean? Bernie is dead. What more can happen to him?"

"He's Jewish, Mabel. That's what's wrong." She moaned, groaned, and blew.

"Flori, since when have you been prejudiced? You've never said anything about anyone's faith or nationality ever in your whole life. After you've met someone you don't even remember if they're black or white."

"Oh no, I don't mean that. How could you even think that? What I mean is, it's against their faith to have the body mutilated. And, they took Bernie to the city to do an autopsy."

"How do you know all this?"

"Well, Jake heard some of the men talking at the café. What do you think will happen now, Mabel?"

I poured two cups of coffee, fixed Flori's up with cream and sugar, and handed it to her.

"I have no idea. Melanie would know what to do. Besides, I don't think Bernie was a practicing Jew, was he?"

"Practicing Jew? I don't think you can say that. It's like saying that I'm a practicing German or American. It's just who they are."

"Well, I don't know about that but anyway, what's going to happen? Are they going to have a funeral?"

"Ben Jacobson says he'll have to have this prayer he called it a Kaddish or something. Also, he said his body should be all covered in water to be cleansed and he should be put in white linen clothing before being buried."

"How does Ben know all this?"

"Well, he really isn't up on all his Jewish rituals so he looked it up on the Internet."

"So, who's going to pray and wash him when he has no family here and his wife is in jail? Besides, everyone thinks that she killed him so they might not think it kosher for her to cleanse his body, right?"

"I know. That's what's so upsetting, Mabel. What's going to happen to Bernie's body? Jewish people bury their dead within a day or two and there's poor Bernie's body way off somewhere in some forensic lab in the city. It's so mortifying."

"Well, I know one thing, Flori. It's not for you or me to decide anything. There's no point in crying over it, is there? There's nothing that you can do."

"I know. I know. The whole thing is very upsetting though." She wiped away some stray tears and wiped where there were no tears in case she missed a few. "I guess you heard Reg had to call in the city cops."

"No, I did not hear that. When were you going to share that bit of information?"

Flori blushed. "Well, if you must know, I wanted to talk about the more important things first. I think Bernie's burial is far more important than who's getting involved in the murder case."

"So, if this is an open and shut case with a confession, why bring in the big guns?"

"Oh Mabel, I don't know. Maybe it's not as open and shut as Reg thinks. Maybe he was having second thoughts about it all. Remember he is planning to retire soon so perhaps this is just too much for him to handle. Jake says he's not looking too good - kind of drained and pale."

I sighed. "I suppose I could give him a call."

"I suppose you couldn't. He'll feel truly embarrassed if he has to ask for your help again. Besides, I think he can handle it without your interference."

"I don't interfere and this is not about Reg's ego; it's about Melanie's life. Do you want an innocent woman going to jail just because it might be upsetting to Reg?"

"Well, it's up to you, Mabel. All I ask is that you don't involve me. By the way, I think you really enjoyed our little jaunt into the city, didn't you? I'm quite looking forward to next Friday's trip, aren't you?"

"It wasn't as bad as I thought it might be. By the way, Flori, did you notice how Calvin was walking when he came back to the bus?"

"I never noticed how he was walking before he got on the bus so why should I worry about how he got off? Why are you so concerned about the way Calvin walks?"

"Oh I'm not really all that concerned, just curious, that's all. Actually, I don't know how he walked when he got on. Miss MJ asked me to watch, that's all."

"Miss MJ? Why in the world would she be worrying about that? She can hardly walk herself. Is that why she was whispering in your ear all the time? I wondered what she was talking about. Who cares how Calvin walks anyway? To tell you the truth, he's about the last person I worry about. I don't think he's a very nice person to hire to take those lovely elderly people to the city. If we hadn't been there, he wouldn't have even helped them on and off. I think I should get Jake to talk to Mr. Kinney about him."

"Well, wait until after next Friday. M J is a smart lady and I want to see what Calvin is up to."

"Oh, for Pete's sake, Mabel, you missed your calling; you should've been born as a bloodhound."

For some reason, Flori struck her own funny bone and she proceeded to laugh until she completely drained her tear ducts. While she was busy with that I washed out our mugs and put on some fresh coffee.

That evening I would give Sheriff Smee a call. I don't care what anyone says, when Reg has nowhere else to turn, he turns to Mabel Wickles.

Chapter Fifteen

I tried phoning Reg that night at home but there was no answer and I definitely wasn't going to call the station. The next day was Saturday, which is my busiest day at the shop. Somehow I would have to figure out how to meet or at least talk to Reg without having to abandon my post. I really need every sale I can make. Flori is always willing to help in time of need but it would depend on the reason. By ten o'clock, I'd seen two unfamiliar patrol cars drive down Main Street so I knew the Parson's Cove police department was off the case. I couldn't help but wonder if Captain Maxymowich had taken Sheriff Smee's place.

It's embarrassing to say but we've had several murders over the past few years in Parson's Cove. Some residents started to call our quiet little town Murder City. I'm sure there were murders in the past but no one seems to remember any of those. Whoever oversees to make sure justice is done in the land, must've thought Reg and his boys needed help so he or she sent out Maxymowich a couple of years ago. He and his crew have returned to Parson's Cove twice since then.

At first, I can honestly say, I had no use for him at all. Maxymowich, that is. He came across as narrow-minded, cold-hearted, and brusque. I didn't even like the way he looked with his white hair slicked straight back, his slouch, and his wrinkled navy suit. After he'd solved the crime, however, the Captain came across as a much different person - almost human. Perhaps, a more accurate statement would be 'after he and I solved the crime.' He always made a point of coming to my house before leaving town to fill in any details and to sit and have a cup of coffee with me. And, of course, to have his favorite strawberry muffins. I didn't really mind him coming if he could solve the crime but it would be rather nice if Parson's Cove could look after and solve its own problems.

My morning was busier than my usual Saturdays because Beth Smee and Myra Wakefield decided that they wanted to start up a small intimate book club.

"What we mean," Myra quietly explained to me. "We don't want all the women in town joining in. Perhaps, only five or six. Do you think you and Flori would like to join? We're going to meet at my house every week and talk about the book that we've read. Then, we'll pass the books around for the next week and see what the other person got out of it. I think it will be such fun." She smiled and winked. "And, of course, there will be wine and cheese. I mean, what's a club without wine and cheese? Right, Mabel?" Another wink.

It wasn't my kind of thing. I'm more into reading and drinking my wine curled up in bed all alone. Besides, she probably invited me because I'd be curious about all the books she was buying. However, I thought Flori would enjoy it, especially the wine and cheese part, so I said, "It sounds interesting. It's something Flori would love. I'm not sure I can make it. It's almost time for taking inventory but when do you meet?"

Beth said, "We're going to get together on Monday nights at Myra's house. Reg is always home that night especially now that Captain Maxymowich is in town, so I want to escape. He's not the easiest person to live with right now."

Before I could ask Beth any questions, Myra said, "Since this is sort of a secret club make sure you don't mention it to anyone, okay, Mabel? Especially Esther. We really don't want her or Millicent coming and spoiling it for the rest of us."

"Trust me, Myra, Esther would be the last person I would tell. No, I'll keep it under my hat. You can ask Flori though - she might like it."

For the next few minutes, I helped them pick out some of the old classics that I have packed away in the back shelves and some of my favorite mysteries. They left happy and I was happy. I'd not only made a big sale, now I knew when I could catch Reg – Monday evening at home.

It was almost four when Flori burst through the door. She entered like a tornado and I knew from the get-go that something terrible had happened. However, it was difficult to tell if she was angry, sad, or her hemorrhoids were acting up again. Anyway, her face was very red and she'd clenched both of her hands into fists. I bet anyone meeting her on the sidewalk either walked to the other side or started running.

"I can't believe it, Mabel. Did you hear the latest about Bernie?"

"Now what? The poor man is dead. He apparently didn't get cleaned up the way he should have and his burial had to wait longer than it should have. What more could happen to the man?"

"The Baptists buried him."

I wasn't quite sure how I was supposed to take this. I knew all of Melanie's family went to the old Baptist church so it wasn't a really huge shock.

"So? Aren't you glad that the poor man finally got to rest in peace? What did you want to happen?"

"They buried his ashes, Mabel." She then burst into tears. I'm sure she'd been saving them up so she could dump all of them on me because there were a lot of them. In between sobs and hiccoughing, she said, "I don't think Jews are supposed to be cremated."

"Here, I bought a fresh box of Kleenex just for you." I took out the little piece of cardboard and handed her the box. "When you're finished you can explain why this has you so upset and why it's any of your business."

Through her sobs and tears, she glared at me. When she finished up she said, "I'll tell you why I'm so upset - I think it's terrible that Melanie's family has taken over and they aren't even considering his faith."

"Perhaps, Flori, this was his wish. Perhaps, he had it all outlined in his Last Will and Testimony. Have you ever thought of that? Maybe he converted to the Baptist religion. I'm sure it happens. And, you think this concerns you because...?"

She stopped sniffling and stared at me. I knew she'd have no answer for that.

"Personally, Flori, I think you are just as curious as me and to be honest with you, I don't think you can mind your own business either."

As you can imagine, I said this in a very soft loving tone. She says it often enough to me but somehow, I've never tried putting it on the other foot. For a brief moment, she was speechless.

She wiped her eyes once more and cleared her throat. "I don't think you quite understand the situation, Miss Wickles. Melanie's family is doing this because they hated Bernie. That's why."

"Flori, that's just crazy. There's no way they would do that for that reason. I'm sure they did it like that because there was no one else to bury him and after all, he is – or was, their son-in-law. Who told you all this nonsense?"

"Denny Wakefield was talking about it at the café. Melanie's brother, Steven, got into a big fight with Bernie not that long ago. He threatened to punch him in the face if he didn't stop treating Melanie so bad." She stopped talking and waited for that information to sink in before she continued, "Were you aware that Bernie used to leave Melanie alone for long periods of time, Mabel? Were you also aware that Melanie was thinking about getting a divorce?"

"No, I can't say that I was aware of that, Flori. If he was mistreating her, she had motive to kill him but if she was divorcing him, why bother? That wouldn't make any sense, would it? On the other hand, if Steven hated him, he might very easily have a motive for murdering him."

Flori smiled. "So, that's probably the reason why Captain Maxymowich sent Melanie home after the funeral."

"What? Why are you just telling me this now, Flori? Are you saying that Melanie is back home? Did Maxymowich drop all the charges? And, how long have you known all this?"

"Don't raise your voice at me, Mabel. The moment I found this out, I rushed right over." She suddenly burst into another torrent of tears and through them she stammered, "I thought you'd be so pleased." She blew her nose. "I don't know why we have all this horrible violence in our town. We never argue about anything except when there's been a crime committed, did you know that, Mabel?"

I didn't have the heart to tell her we'd argued the night before about when the Post Office had been built. Flori and I argue constantly. Perhaps, it's done with more passion when someone's been murdered.

"I'm sorry. I should know you'd come right over to tell me. Did Denny happen to say why Melanie was sent home?"

"Apparently her confession didn't sound believable. That's what Denny told Jake anyway."

"I'm wondering how come Denny knows all this?"

"It's because Myra and Beth are good friends and I guess Reg told Beth. At least, that's what I figure."

"Then Denny tells Jake and Jake tells you."

Flori beamed through her tears, "And I tell you, Mabel."

"All right," I said. "I have to think of what to do next." I should've said this to myself but unfortunately, it was said aloud.

"What you have to do? You don't have to do anything. How many police officers do you think it takes to solve a murder? The town is brimming with them so I doubt they need any help from you."

I patted her on the arm. "You're right, Flori. I don't know what I was thinking. I happen to find mysteries so intriguing, don't you?"

"No. I find them very upsetting. By the way, I found something else out. The bus is going to the city on Wednesday. I don't know why it's so soon but it's okay with us, right? I told Mr. Kinney that it was. I'm so looking forward to it, aren't you?"

Blast! I'd forgotten to ask Delores if she could watch the store on Friday and now, I'd have to ask for Wednesday. I guess deep in my heart I was hoping the whole thing would blow over and I'd get out of going. Oh well, there was always Miss Smith - she and I could watch Calvin and check out his walk. I wouldn't mind knowing where he disappeared to as well. He was up to something no good.

Flori left for home and a few minutes later, Esther walked in. At least once a week, she does this to me.

She comes in at the last minute forcing me to keep the store open and then she leaves without buying anything. It sends me home in a foul mood and she knows it.

Once again, she was in this cheery mood and it was extremely irritating.

Chapter Sixteen

Sunday arrived, bleak and cold. Not like a winter cold but anything less than seventy was beginning to make people shiver. It was a welcome reprieve, however. I opened up all my windows and let every room air out, even my sewing room, which hides my gin cache. About an hour later, it started to rain so I had to close it all up again. By that time, all the cats were sitting on the back step waiting for me to let them in. I wasn't quite ready for them yet so they sat and complained. About ten-thirty Flori popped in for a cup of coffee. She brought along two cinnamon buns. When Flori brings two buns it might sound like she's skimping but trust me, she isn't. Each bun was at least eight inches across and the cream cheese icing was about an inch thick. After eating one of those and drinking three cups of coffee, I didn't even want to think about eating or drinking for a few days.

"So, what's on your agenda for today?" she asked, as she wiped icing off her chin. Flori does this with her finger and slides it up into her mouth. She doesn't waste a drop. Unfortunately, I wasted my dribblings in a paper napkin.

I glanced out the window. The rain had stopped and it looked like the skies were clearing. "I don't know. There's always something to do around here; maybe I'll stay in and do some cleaning."

Flori looked at me as if I were mad (that is, the old English meaning).

"Really? You're going to stay inside and clean? I thought you did your cleaning on Mondays now that your shop is closed."

Everything closes down on Monday in Parson's Cove – the bank, the stores and even the library. Not that it was always like this. It used to be that everything stayed open and heaven forbid you even be late for work. I used to go to the shop if I were half dead because if I didn't have a really good reason, Patty Morgan would write it up in the Parson's Cove Weekly, which was all of four pages long. Last year I decided that I was tired of sitting all day every Monday in my shop without one customer coming in so I hung a sign up in the window saying *Closed Mondays*. The next week, the town council met and passed an ordinance declaring Mondays in Parson's Cove, a holiday.

"Naw, I think I'll do some cleaning and maybe bake up some muffins."

Flori gave me her 'knowing' look. "Oh, silly me, I forgot Captain Maxymowich is in town." She stood up. "I think I'd best be going so you can get on with your baking, Mabel."

"Flori, I really didn't even think of him. It's just that I haven't baked in ages and my freezer needs replenishing. For almost three weeks it was too hot to even turn on the top burner of the stove, let alone the oven."

Flori traipsed to the door. "Well, say hello to the good Captain for me."

Not that I'd admit it to Flori but she was right. If Maxymowich did happen to drop in, I should make sure I had some muffins for him. The last time he dropped by after we'd finished solving a case, Reg devoured all of my muffins. That's the hazards of solving a murder with him. This also reminded me that if we were on speaking terms again, I should have some ready for him, too.

The few bags I happened to dig up from the bottom of the freezer had freezer burn so I threw them out. Not until after I'd received my cats' approval, however. I put one down on the floor and each one came over to sniff and walk away. Teddy, one of the male cats, tried batting it with his paw but lost interest after a few pats and the muffin didn't roll.

So, I spent Sunday morning, vacuuming up cat hair, cleaning out boxes of cat litter and baking four dozen strawberry and blueberry muffins. Two dozen of each. I'd picked the berries only weeks before at one of the farms not far away and froze them immediately so they were very fresh. After eating Flori's cinnamon bun and then two muffins, I knew there was a need to go for a long walk. It's my belief if you're going for a walk, there might as well be some purpose to it. Otherwise, to my way of thinking - you're not walking, you're meandering.

It isn't the best manners to just pop into someone's place, especially on a Sunday afternoon but I knew there was someone who wouldn't mind at all. I was sure Charlie Thompson would be sitting on the library bench and I wanted to know if he had any more information for me.

The sun was now peeking out and it was turning into one of those perfect weather days. I could see Charlie's red plaid shirt from two blocks away.

He didn't look up until I called out, "Hey, Charlie, how are you today?"

I did note a slight hint of a smile on his lips, which is a good sign when it comes to Charlie.

"Mind if I sit down?" I never wait for an answer. I sat down beside him and didn't say anything. I could see why he liked sitting here. Not that I would want to, day after day after day, but it is a good spot for seeing almost everything that goes on, on Main Street in Parson's Cove.

"You want to know more about the mystery?" he asked after about five minutes of silence.

I didn't want to appear too anxious. "Only if you wish to divulge it, Charlie. Do you know anything more? Do you think that it had something to do with Bernie's murder?"

He shrugged.

"Does that mean you might know more or you don't know if it had anything to do with the murder?"

Charlie frowned. "You ask such hard questions, Mabel. All I know is what I've seen."

"What did you see? Is it something we should go to the police about, Charlie?"

He shrugged and then shook his head. "Not enough evidence."

The secret to discussing ideas with Charlie is never to lose your patience.

"Can you tell me what you saw?"

He started to rock back and forth so I knew he was getting nervous.

"It was dark. Very dark, but I saw the taxi parked behind Scooter's garage."

At that point, Charlie closed down. His rocking increased and I knew if I didn't leave, he'd become more agitated. Since he's my eyes and ears in the night I want to keep those lines of communication open – even if the lines are very short.

This really didn't seem like much information. I mean, why shouldn't Calvin be visiting Scooter Macalvey? I'm sure they've been friends for years. For all I knew, they could've been staying up half the night playing poker.

Scooter repairs shoes in his garage. I personally don't know how he survives on what he makes. No one gets his or her shoes repaired anymore. It's just as cheap to buy a new pair. Some of the older ones still like to take their shoes to him though. Scooter's wife, Betty, works in the kitchen at the hospital so I imagine she's the one who puts most of the food on the table. Sometimes I walk down the back lane, usually looking for a cat or two, and I've seen the huge garden they have. Scooter must look after it when he's not replacing heels on someone's shoes. Come to think of it, he might not be doing too good a job as it was growing pretty wild the last time I gave it a glance.

I started for home I admit a bit disappointed. The town was so quiet. I didn't see any police cars anywhere – not Reg and his boys, nor Captain Maxymowich and his boys. What was happening with this murder case anyway? Was Melanie really the killer after all? Was her brother the killer? On the other hand, were there things about Bernie that we didn't know? It wouldn't be the first time that someone in Parson's Cove was leading a double life.

The only person walking down the street was Amy Hunter. She was taking her little Pekingese for a walk. It suddenly hit me that Murray McFerguson wouldn't be able to do that anymore. When I'd been down on the beach and looked at the back of his house, it was so quiet and lifeless looking. Perhaps it would be good to drop in to make a quick visit. After all, he was the one who lost two friends: one human and one canine. I could drop off some muffins for them.

I was looking forward to Monday. Hunting for clues in solving a murder is almost as exciting as the moment that you know who did it. One thing for sure - I was certainly looking forward to Monday much more than Wednesday. This was going to be the last time I would go to the city with those old codgers. I would invite Flori over after supper for a nice glass of wine and break the news to her.

Chapter Seventeen

Monday morning was clear and bright. The sun shone, the birds sang, and my cats couldn't wait to get outside. For a brief two hours or so they could pretend to be searching for their food in the wilds of Africa. As I watched from the kitchen window, I was sure the birds were getting a kick out of it too. Sammy, my only white cat, sat under a tree branch, his body literally trembling with anticipation. The branch was about six feet above him but he bravely kept leaping into the air. The bird never moved but simply looked down at him and fluttered its wings.

It was nine and I was almost as excited as Sammy was. Surely today I would find more clues to Bernie's murder.

I was glad now that I'd baked some fresh muffins. Erma met me at the door. She looked like she hadn't slept in days but she cheered up a little when she saw the muffins. Erma isn't quite as big as Flori but almost. Like Flori, she has a contagious laugh. I always enjoy it when she comes into the store. She's the type of person who can find something to laugh about in almost any situation. It looked as if she was having a hard time finding anything to smile about this time.

"Erma, I wanted to come by and see how you folks are doing." I handed her the bag with the muffins in it. "This must be an awful time for Murray. I know how much he loved that old dog and how close he was to Bernie too. How is he doing?"

Erma stood back and motioned me inside. We stood in her living room.

"I don't know what to do, Mabel. Come and look at him."

I followed her through the house and into the kitchen. She stopped at the window.

"See him there?"

I stood on my tiptoes and looked out. Murray was sitting in a chair at the back end of the property apparently watching the lake.

"I see him but what's wrong? Why don't you like him sitting by the water? Don't you think it's good for him?"

"At first, I did. In fact, I'm the one who suggested it but now it's out of hand, Mabel. He sits out there staring into space all day long. He doesn't even come in to eat. If I didn't take his food out to him I think he'd starve to death. I'm at my wit's end. Would you go and talk to him?"

It was a strange request since I never really ever talk to Murray. Not that I don't say hello when I pass him on the street but I've never had any reason to strike up a conversation. Now to start communicating with someone who's lost his best friend and his dog by the same murder weapon is something entirely different.

"Please?" Erma looked so desperate that before I thought of what I was doing, I smiled, nodded, and walked out the back door onto the deck and down the lawn to see Murray. I had no idea what I was going to say. This is one reason why I stay away from funerals. Some people are good at condolences but not me. If I do go to a funeral, I go with Flori and Jake. That way I can stand beside them and nod. I've even had bereaved folks send me a thank you card for the thoughtful expressions that I shared with them. All that for just a nod.

The closer I got, the more I realized what bad shape Murray was in. He didn't even hear me coming and when I said his name, he looked up as if he was seeing an apparition. Like he didn't know who I was.

"Murray," I said. "It's me, Mabel Wickles."

It took a few seconds to register.

"Oh, Mabel. You'll find Erma in the house." He turned and continued looking out through the trees to the lake as if this was a very important job or something.

I plunked down on the grass beside him. If he noticed he didn't let on.

"I've already been in to see Erma."

As if seeing me again for the first time, he said, "Oh, that's nice." He kept staring into space as if I wasn't there.

"Murray," I said. "I came to offer my condolences. I'm so sorry to hear about Bernie and about your old dog, Biscuit. You must be devastated."

He nodded and tears sprang into his eyes.

"He didn't have to do it."

"He? Whom do you mean, Murray? You mean the person who killed Bernie or the one who killed Biscuit?"

He hesitated for a moment and I saw another emotion cross over his face. Anger. It was only for a second and if I'd glanced away for that long, I would've missed it. In fact it was so intense, it was much more than anger – it was a mixture of rage and hatred. This was something new. Murray always seemed to be as laid back as that old dog of his. Not that I see him on a regular basis but if someone in Parson's Cove has any type of problem, be it alcohol abuse, soap opera addiction or anger management, everyone knows about it. Of course, he had every right to be so angry.

His face softened and tears welled up in his eyes.

"I loved that old dog, Mabel. He never did anyone any harm. There was no reason for him to kill old Biscuit."

"Him? Who's 'him?'"

Murray looked up at me. "Him is the s.o.b who threw a brick at my dog and killed him. That's who 'him' is. Anybody who does something like that deserves to die himself."

"What if it was a 'she?' Melanie claims to have killed Bernie. Maybe Biscuit was there and in her anger, she picked up the brick and threw it at Biscuit too. You know, sort of like two birds with one stone."

He shook his head. "Bernie could be a jerk and I'm sure Melanie felt like killing him sometimes but she would never kill a dog. Besides, Biscuit was killed out in that empty field."

"But what if whoever killed Bernie took the dog and dumped him in the field?"

He looked up at me with a puzzled look. "Why would a person do that?"

"I don't know. It just seems to me that if they were both killed by the same brick, they must've been together at the time. What if Biscuit saw her killing Bernie and he attacked her? Even the meekest dogs will protect people, you know."

He shook his head again. "No. Biscuit would never attack. He was the sweetest dog in the world. It was some stranger who did it. Some deranged stranger."

"How do you know that? Why would some deranged stranger kill Bernie and your dog?"

If I'd thrown ice-cold water in his face, I couldn't have received a more shocking reaction. For one brief moment I thought he was going to jump off that lawn chair and sock me in the jaw. He did literally lift himself off about five inches. That was enough to make me stand up and very quickly for someone with arthritic knees.

With his fist and his teeth clenched, he yelled, "Get off my property, Mabel Wickles, if you know what's good for you. Don't I have enough to worry about than having you poking around here in my business?"

When someone uses that tone with me, I don't dilly-dally. I headed back to the house as fast as my short legs would take me. Erma was waiting on the deck by the back door.

"See, I told you." She plucked a used tissue from her apron pocket and dabbed at her nose. Her eyes were red from crying. "I don't know what I'm going to do with him, Mabel. He's heartbroken over that old dog of his. If he'd died of old age, I don't think it would be so hard on Murray. And, losing Bernie too – he just can't handle it all."

"Has he talked to you about Bernie in the past few weeks or so? Did he tell you if Bernie and Melanie were having any trouble?"

"Trouble? What do you mean 'trouble?' Are you talking about what Prunella overheard? Because if that's what you're referring to, I wouldn't put much faith in it." She held the door open for me and followed right behind. It banged shut. She motioned to one of her kitchen chairs for me to sit. "I never knew this but, Mabel, Prunella has been a secret drunk for years. Someone was telling me that all she does is sit on her porch and drink margaritas." She pulled two mugs down from the lower shelf of her cupboard and filled them with coffee. "Cream and sugar?" Before I could answer, she took a carton of milk from the fridge and put the sugar bowl in front of me. We shared one spoon for stirring. Erma peered at me over her cup. "Why would you ask if Murray talked about Bernie and Melanie? I'm sure he doesn't know anything about their private life. Bernie used to go fishing with Murray but it seemed Bernie was busy lately. Excuse my French but that sort of pissed Murray off a little. I mean, friendship is something special. After so many years, you don't just drop someone. Right, Mabel? I know one thing for sure you wouldn't drop Flori, would you?"

I couldn't imagine dropping Flori, as Melanie put it. However, if Flori happened to be spending more time with other people than with me, would I drop her then? That, of course, was very hypothetical because Flori would never do that.

"I wasn't thinking about what Prunella said, Erma, I was wondering about what Murray said. He told me that Melanie might have felt like killing Bernie sometimes."

Her coffee cup stopped in midair. "He told you that? Are you sure you heard right, Mabel? I know you've been having trouble seeing lately, do you think you might be getting hard of hearing, too?"

"Trust me I have no trouble hearing or seeing for that matter."

"Oh, I thought Flori mentioned something to me about your eyes. I could be wrong."

"You're not wrong. Flori is. For some reason she thinks my eyesight is getting bad but trust me, Erma, I can still see and hear very well. That's why I know what Murray said to me. He said that Melanie probably felt like murdering Bernie sometimes."

"He said, 'murder?'"

"Well, if he didn't say 'murder,' he said 'kill' and that's the same word in my vocabulary."

She drained her coffee, refilled both our cups and put two muffins on a plate.

"Have a muffin. I know I won't be able to get Murray to eat and I don't want to eat alone." We sat for several minutes, silently eating and drinking. "I don't know what to say, Mabel. I have no idea what was going on with Bernie and Murray. For sure, I don't know what was happening with Bernie and Melanie. I thought they were a normal married couple. Melanie never mentioned anything to me. That's why I didn't believe all those things that Prunella was saying – you know, Melanie threatening to kill him. That didn't make any sense. Let's face it, even if you might threaten it but if you were really going to do it, you wouldn't shout it out on the street for everyone to hear, right?"

I shook my head. My mouth was full.

"I honestly have no idea what Murray was talking about." She popped the last of the muffin in her mouth. "These are really good."

"You've never had one of my muffins before?"

Erma thought for a moment and then shook her head.

"You want me to try to find out what Murray was talking about, Mabel?"

"If you can."

"I'll work on it."

"And, I was wondering, Erma, where did Murray find Biscuit?"

"Oh, didn't you hear? Some kids found him in the vacant lot across from Krueger's old house. I guess they were tramping through the empty lot and almost tripped over him. He'd been gone for most of the day but he sometimes would go out on his own. He always came back home so Murray wasn't worried. The boys were very upset. You know, most kids have never seen anything dead."

"What about the brick? Where was the brick?"

She shrugged. "I don't know."

It was almost noon but I wanted to talk to Prunella before I went home. It seemed the whole town was now aware that she had a drinking problem. I doubted that she'd been a secret drinker all the time though. Well, let's face it; I was a secret drinker. I'm sure there's a difference between being a secret drinker and a secret drunk. Of course, I had seven cats to talk to while I was sipping my gin. However, I'm sure Flori wouldn't consider that as not drinking alone.

Prunella wasn't sitting out on her veranda so I went around to the back door. Everything was very quiet. Her flowers in the front and along the side of the house were looking droopy and there was a nice variety of weeds competing for space. Usually Prunella is out weeding, watering and pruning every day. After all, her last name is Flowers and as she jokes, 'she has to live up to her name.'

The inside door was closed so I opened the screen door and knocked. There was no answer. I opened the door and yelled Prunella's name. There was no answer except I thought I heard something like a low moaning sound. That was enough for me. I went inside. The kitchen was a mess. The rum bottle on the kitchen counter was still there but now empty. Or, perhaps it was a new one.

I called again and this time followed the sound. It took me to a small bedroom off a short hallway. Prunella was there, sprawled out on her bed. If she hadn't moaned, I would've pronounced her dead on the spot. Her eyes were open but unseeing. Her one arm hung over the side of the bed. The white sheet had more color in it than her skin did. Except for the bright red. The blood seeping from the side of her head onto the pillow.

I didn't waste time searching for a pulse. I raced back to her kitchen and dialed 911.

Chapter Eighteen

Hermann Wheeler must've been sitting in the ambulance because within seconds I could hear his siren wailing. I made sure to say that I thought Prunella was dead because then Doc Fritz would come. There was no way I wanted Hermann trying to do CPR on Prunella. Or, on any other living thing for that matter.

I waited for them on the front veranda where just days before Prunella had enjoyed her 'iced tea.' Seemed hard to imagine she might be the next victim in Parson's Cove. If she died we would have two murders to solve.

The ambulance flew into Prunella's narrow driveway and skidded to a stop. The siren howled to an end as if being let out of its misery and both men jumped out and bolted for the front door.

"Get out of the way," Hermann yelled, almost knocking me over with the gurney he was trying to hold under his arm and drag along at the same time.

"Show me where she is," Fritzy shouted and whipped out in front of Hermann.

I hurried ahead of the doctor not wanting to be side swiped by the gurney and showed him into Prunella's bedroom. I have to admit the old doctor went right into action. From where I stood Prunella looked very dead but Fritzy must've found a pulse or some sign of life because within seconds he said, "Wheeler, get that gurney over here and let's get her to the hospital."

"Is she alive?" I asked.

"Barely," is all he said.

The two of them gently moved her onto the gurney, which was no small feat in such a narrow space, and Hermann wrapped her in a gray blanket.

Neither man said anything to each other or to me until I started to climb into the ambulance. Then, Fritz said, "What do you think you're doing, Wickles?"

Before I could explain that Prunella might like a friend along with her, the door slammed shut in my face.

It was probably best that I didn't accompany the ambulance to the hospital because I realized I had only a short period of time to check the house for clues before the police arrived. By police, it would undoubtedly mean Captain Maxymowich and not Reg Smee.

I figured the intruder would go in through the back door so I went around to the back of the house. It's so much easier to solve a crime in a city because if the door isn't bashed in, it means the victim knew the intruder. In Parson's Cove, however, no one ever locks their doors so it could be a neighbor or serial killer. Besides, if there were any footprints or anything like that, they would be mine anyway.

This time I stood back and took a good look around the kitchen. Someone had been to visit Prunella. There were two glasses on the table. One was empty but there was a small amount of light brown liquid in the other one. The empty one was where Prunella sat when I'd visited her and knowing how much she liked her rum and coke, I assumed the empty one was hers. I bent over to smell the contents in the other glass. It was Prunella's drink of choice all right. I hoped that Maxymowich could get some prints off it.

One thing that I found puzzling was how Prunella got to the bedroom. Had her assailant hit her and then dragged her to the bedroom or was she there when he or she assaulted her? If she were dragged, some furniture or perhaps one of her shoes or something would've been found on the floor. It was hard to tell because Hermann's gurney had knocked half the furniture down on the way to the bedroom. What he didn't knock over on the way in, he did on the way out.

I went into the bedroom. As much as I hated snooping through Prunella's things, I knew it was necessary. There was only one large dresser along one wall. There really wasn't room for any more furniture. I opened each of the drawers to made a quick search. Nothing drew my attention until I opened the last drawer, which hadn't been shut properly. On the bottom in plain sight, I found a brown leather zippered case. Inside that case, I found a roll of money and a small packet filled with white powder.

I was standing there, staring at the case when Captain Maxymowich walked into the room.

Chapter Nineteen

To say that I jumped ten feet into the air wouldn't be much of an exaggeration. How anyone could sneak up like that without making a sound is surely a talent. He stood staring at me but I couldn't utter a sound until my heart stopped hammering.

When I finally regained my normalcy, all I could do was babble, "I wasn't going to steal this money, Captain Maxymowich. I happened to open the drawer, which by the way, wasn't closed properly and there it was. I'm sure it isn't stolen though. This packet of white stuff? I know there's an explanation. I know Prunella and she isn't a drug addict. She might drink a bit too much now and again but she's been going through a lot of stress. Well, if you saw her at the hospital you'd know how much stress she's going through. I have no idea who beat her up. She was in bed already when I got here. If I hadn't heard her moan, I would never have walked right in. Do you think it has something to do with Bernie's murder? This vicious assault on Prunella? I mean, she's the one who witnessed Bernie and Melanie fighting."

I said all that without taking a breath. (Try reading it without taking a breath.)

"Are you finished, Mabel?"

"I reckon I am."

"That's good because I'll take that roll of money from you and that packet that you have in your other hand." He turned to the uniformed cop who'd come up behind him. "Could you escort Miss Wickles out the back door?"

"You don't have to escort me. I can find my way, Captain."

"No problem." He smiled. Literally, smiled. "We don't want you to get sidetracked on the way out."

He relieved me of the money, pouch, and packet. The slightly overweight balding officer took my elbow and steered me through the hallway, the kitchen and then out the back door. I'm not saying that the man shoved me out the door but I did feel some pressure in the small of my back.

By the time I reached the gate, there was another cop car pulling up. I was pleased to see that one of them was a woman. I gave her a big smile in case we happened to meet up again and I needed someone to stand up for me.

I could hear my phone ringing before I opened the door. The answering machine was blinking too so I figured it was Flori. I grabbed it on the fourth ring.

Before I could say a word, Flori was yelling, "Mabel, where have you been? I've been calling all morning. I even sent Jake over to look for you and he said you weren't home so I asked Delores to search your house. She said you weren't there. Where the heck were you?"

"Wait a minute, you sent Jake over?"

"Yes, I did. I also asked him to go back and look inside your house too but he wouldn't. I told him that you could be lying dead on the floor but he still wouldn't look. Where were you anyway?"

"And you sent Delores over to search through my house?"

"Well, what was I supposed to do? No one answered my calls and I phoned several times. Where the heck were you?"

I looked at my answering machine. "You didn't phone several times, Flori; you phoned exactly nine times. That goes beyond 'several.'"

There was silence on the other end.

"That's a lot of times, Flori."

"Where were you, Mabel?"

"Well, as a matter of fact, I had a couple of places to go. They probably wouldn't interest you, Flori."

"If you don't tell me right now, I'm going to come over with Jake's old shotgun and blow your living room window out."

"You have never threatened me before."

"You have never irritated me so much before, Mabel. It isn't a joke. I always worry about you - especially if I hear sirens ringing. I know I don't need to know your every move but I feel much better when I do."

There was a sniff and I knew I'd better start talking before the tears erupted.

"I'm sorry, Flori. I really do wish you wouldn't worry about me so much. I'm sure I told you that I was going over to visit Erma and Murray. I feel so sorry for them. Murray isn't doing too well, you know. It must be awful to have your best friend and your dog both clobbered by the same brick. And, both die. I took some muffins over for them. I think Erma really appreciated my visit. Murray's pretty much a basket case right now. All he does is sit and stare at the lake. Do you think Jake would go and visit him, Flori?"

There was a brief pause.

"No, you didn't, Mabel."

"Didn't what?"

"Tell me that you were going over to Erma and Murray's place."

"Really? I'm sorry. I thought I had. Did I tell you that I was going to stop in and visit Prunella?"

"You went to visit Prunella? Why, on earth, would you do that? She's drunk half the time, Mabel. You'd better stay away from her."

"You know what, Flori? I want to thank you for sending Delores over to check out my house. You know why?"

"No of course I don't. I have no idea how your brain works."

"Because no one answered when I knocked on Prunella's door but guess what?"

"Mabel, I am not going to guess." She let out a very loud sigh. "Come to think of it, I will guess. You found her body bludgeoned to death on the kitchen floor. No wait, someone had shot her right through her kitchen window. Or, let's see, perhaps, someone shot her with a poisoned dart."

"Did someone already tell you?"

"What? Tell me what? Someone shot Prunella with a poisoned dart? Are you serious, Mabel? Oh my heavens, what is this world coming to?"

I'm sure all the deaf people in the nursing home four blocks away from Flori's house could hear the wail that she let out. Sammy, my cat, jumped down from the chair where he'd been sound asleep, gave me a disgusted look and walked into the living room.

I waited for those few seconds when she had to inhale and catch her breath.

"No, Flori, she wasn't hit with a dart but she was beaten up. That's what I meant. Did you know that someone hit her on the side of the head and that she's now in the hospital?"

Whispering replaced wailing.

"Someone hit Prunella?"

"Yes, and I'm wondering if she'll make it. I thought she was dead. If I hadn't heard that soft moaning, I never would've gone inside to check things out."

"And that's why you're glad I sent Delores over to your house? You think there's someone who's planning on beating you up too?"

"No, Flori. I'm glad because I like knowing you keep check on me. I'm sure if someone were out to murder me, whomever you sent over would find me before the end came."

"What end?"

"The end when I died."

The wrong wording but it was too late to try to mend it. I waited until I was quite sure my dear friend was finished weeping.

"What I'm saying, Flori, is that I'm not upset that you sent Delores over to search my house. I'm glad because if something had happened to me, like a heart attack or something, she could call for the ambulance – like I called the ambulance for Prunella."

"All right. I'm glad you're glad. Can we change the subject now, Mabel?"

"Of course, we can. What did you want to talk about?"

"I can understand you wanting to visit Erma but why would you visit Prunella?"

"Somehow this doesn't seem like we're changing the subject, Flori, but that's okay. I wanted to see how she was doing. That's all. No big deal."

"Well, that's very nice of you. Are you coming to the little book club meeting tonight?"

"No but that's okay, Flori, I know it's something you'll enjoy."

"Myra said you were taking inventory? Since when do you take inventory this time of year?"

"I thought I might get a head start on it, that's all."

"That's a really big head start, Mabel. You don't have to make up some excuse. Not everyone wants to read books when it's ninety degrees outside, you know. I'm not fussy about it myself."

"The wine and cheese might be good though."

"That's what I'm counting on."

We shared a good belly laugh and hung up.

I have to admit that although I didn't lie, I did intentionally leave out the part where I was planning on visiting Sheriff Smee while Flori was sitting and enjoying that wine and cheese.

Chapter Twenty

Reg was definitely not looking his best when he answered the door. For example, last year when he had an abscessed tooth and I paid a visit, he looked much better. And, happier. At least, then he took the time to comb his hair. Not that he has much hair left to comb but what was there, was standing straight up. I was also not that impressed on how far he opened the door. All he did was stick his head out.

"What do you want, Mabel?"

"That's the way you greet a neighbor who's come visiting?"

"That's the way I greet Mabel Wickles when she comes visiting. Now, what do you want?"

"Well, I wouldn't mind coming in. I brought you some of your favorite muffins, I'll have you know. I haven't seen you round in ages and I thought you might be missing your usual coffee and muffins. Well, I didn't bring over any coffee but we could drink some of yours, I suppose."

"Beth isn't here - although I have a feeling you already knew that. You've come to get information about the murder, right?" He gave a little grunt-like laugh. "Well, you've come to the wrong place. I probably know less than you do. In fact, I would bet on it."

He started to close the door but as usual I'm prepared for such things so I stuck my foot out before it went shut.

"Hey," I screamed. "You smashed my foot."

The door swung open again.

"Mabel, I can't believe you'd stoop so low as to put your foot in the door."

I bent down and unlaced my sneaker. My entire foot was on fire.

"I think you broke my foot, Reg." I gently removed the shoe and then my sock. "Well, at least, there's no blood."

"That was the stupidest thing I've ever seen. What did you do that for?" He kneeled down to have a better look. "It doesn't look broken to me. See if you can wiggle your toes."

All five wiggled without any problem. I didn't mention it but the foot was also pain-free already.

"I hope you don't mind, Reg," I said. "I think maybe I'd better sit down and rest my foot for a few minutes. I'm sure if I walk on it right now, it will just irritate it and I'll really suffer for it later on."

"I suppose you should."

He looked about as enthused as my cats do when I fill their bowls with generic dried cat food.

"I told you that my wife isn't home, Mabel. I don't think it would look right if I had you come inside. Maybe if you walk home slowly, it won't be so bad. Sometimes exercise is the best thing for injuries."

I looked down at my foot. "No, I can't walk home on it just yet, Reg." I smiled up at him. "I know what we could do though." I pointed to the two lawn chairs tucked under the patio table. "We could sit here and talk while my foot recovers from the smashing you gave it."

Reg's eyes rolled up but I paid no attention.

"Why don't we sit here for a few minutes? You could enjoy one of your muffins, if you like. I'll have a cup of coffee if you have one on. If not, it's okay."

"No, Mabel, we don't keep coffee brewing all day here. If you want, you can have a beer. That's what I'm going to have. Well? Do you want one or not?"

I'm not a beer drinker but it was warm out, I was thirsty, and I did want to keep Reg talking as long as I could.

I nodded. "Sounds good to me."

He disappeared into the house before I could ask for a glass and napkin.

A few minutes later the sheriff returned carrying two beers in one hand and the bag of muffins in the other. He placed one bottle in front of me and the other with the muffins, in front of himself. I watched in amazement as he tipped the bottle and drained half of it. After placing it back on the table, he wiped his hand down the front of his shirt. Somehow, I think there should be stricter rules on beer drinking etiquette.

While Reg was tearing into his first muffin, I gently picked up the cold bottle of beer and took my first drink. The bottle dripped with so much sweat that it almost slid right through my hand. After the first swallow of that ice-cold brew, I totally understood beer drinking etiquette. I wiped my wet hand down my pant leg, took a good grip on the bottle and tilted it up. The more that went down, the thirstier I became. After four generous gulps, I came up for air. Two seconds later, a belch erupted from somewhere inside of me and blasted out of my mouth with enough force to make me almost fall out of the chair. Fortunately, since Reg is well acquainted with the rituals of beer drinking, he didn't bat an eye.

I waited until Reg had devoured two muffins before I said, "I imagine you heard about Prunella?"

"Prunella?" His beer was now finished but he still had muffins to go. "What about Prunella?"

"You didn't hear that someone beat her up and she's in the hospital?"

Sheriff Smee stared at me. He was silent for several seconds. There was shock in his face but also a look of sadness.

"Nobody told me, Mabel." He quickly stood up. "I'll be right back."

He returned with two more beers and stood one in front of me. I made no protest but quickly downed the small portion I still had left. Flori would never forgive me for this.

"So, tell me about it. How do you know? Is Maxymowich keeping in contact with you now instead of me?"

I shook my head. "No, it's just that I'm the one who found her. That's why I know."

"You found Prunella? Where?"

"Well, I went to her place and when she didn't answer, I opened the door and called. I heard someone moaning so I went into her bedroom and there she was. I thought she was dead. She was just lying there, staring up at the ceiling and there was blood all over the side of her head. I called the ambulance and after Fritzy and Herman took her away, I checked out her house. At least as much as I could before Maxymowich arrived."

"Hmmm. So they didn't even call the local sheriff. How do you like that, Mabel?"

"I personally think it's totally unfair. To tell you the truth, Reg, I think you and I could solve this murder faster than any of those city cops could. Anyway, guess what I found at Prunella's?"

He smiled. "So, you think that you and I could solve this case?"

"Of course, I do. We've solved other cases, haven't we? Why couldn't we solve this one?"

"Without Captain Maxymowich finding out?"

"Obviously, it would have to be done very discreetly. But, Reg, don't you want to know what I found at Prunella's?"

He tipped his bottle and I waited.

"You win. What did you find at Prunella's? Couldn't be the murder weapon because I have that here."

"You have the brick that killed Bernie here? Like, right here in your house?"

He nodded. "Yep. I was the one who sent it to the lab for prints and I'm the one they returned it to. It is now in my safekeeping until the trial."

"Does Maxy know?"

Another guzzle. "Yeah. Had to tell him. The only reason it's here is because there weren't any prints on it at all. Everything was all smudged." He laughed. "Wasn't that generous of him? Leave something with the old sheriff to guard so he'll feel important. Hey, I know – how about something that means nothing." With that, he tipped the bottle up and drained it.

"Can I see it?"

"You want to see the brick?"

I nodded.

Reg shook his head and grinned. "Mabel," he said, "You're a bit on the morbid side, you know that?"

"You know I am, Reg. I'd like to have a look, that's all."

He hauled himself off the chair with a few more grunts than were necessary. However, when a person is full of self-pity, I've found he tends to do that.

"Okey-dokey, Mabel. You sit tight and I'll bring the brick out for you to see. Mind you, you can't touch it." He stopped and looked at me. "You're sure you want to? I mean, most ladies get a little skittish around murder weapons." Then, as if he'd told the funniest joke in the world, he burst out laughing.

"Oh right, that's only ladies. But, Mabel, you're one of the best old girls there is."

I watched as our noble sheriff turned and walked a bit unsteadily towards the door. If he returned with more beer instead of the brick, I would have to as nonchalantly as possible, knock them over and spill all the beer. Sheriff Smee was definitely past his limit.

Thankfully, he returned with only the brick. A heavy clear plastic bag with information attached protected the brick inside. Reg handed it to me and sat down.

"There it is, Mabel. An ordinary red brick. The kind you see all over Parson's Cove. You know how I know? I went into every yard in this town and checked them out."

"What about the blood? They identified it? It was Bernie's?"

"Yep, it was Bernie's all right. And, Biscuit's."

"Could they tell who was killed first?"

"Oh, they're a smart bunch, Mabel. The dog was killed first but not by much." He took the package and pulled the plastic tight so I could see the dark dried blood. "They can tell it's a dog's blood and they can tell that Biscuit was probably killed about an hour before Bernie."

I stared at him. "Biscuit was killed about an hour before Bernie?"

"That's right."

"So, there goes my theory out the window."

"What was your theory? You figured someone was attacking Bernie and the dog interfered and ended up dead too and then the murderer dumped the dog?"

I nodded. "That's pretty much my theory. That seemed to fit somehow. Now I have to get my head around the dog being hit on the head before Bernie. Why? Who would murder a lazy sweet dog like Biscuit? I don't even think he barked, did he?"

"Not much. I hear Murray is devastated. Erma was talking to Beth about him. Beth thought it would help if Erma joined this book club thing so she invited her." He shrugged and tipped his empty beer bottle up. There must've been a couple of drops because he smacked his lips. I could see him eyeing my half-empty bottle so I tipped it up and guzzled the whole thing down. I'm learning that I should not do this because I'm sure I swallow half a bottle of air with it. The wind that blew out from my mouth and nose when I was finished almost knocked the empty bottle down.

Reg smiled with appreciation. "You sure know how to drink beer, Mabel. Can't get Beth to join me for some reason. Course, she does like a nice glass of white wine once in awhile." He drifted off into a momentary dream world. I imagine thinking about Beth either daintily sipping her white wine or letting out an earsplitting belch.

I stood up. "Well, I guess I'd better be heading home, Reg."

He looked down at my feet. "Might be a good idea to put your sock and shoe back on."

"Oops. Guess I'm not used to downing two bottles of beer so fast." I sat back down and pulled on my sock and shoe.

"You never told me what you found at Prunella's place, Mabel. Actually, you never even said if she was dead or alive. I'm surmising that she must be alive, right?"

"Oh yeah, I guess I got distracted with that brick." I stayed sitting. "I hope Prunella will be okay. She looked like she was dead to me but Fritzy got there in time."

"She's going to want to thank you for saving her life, that's for sure. You did a good thing, Mabel. So, what did you find in her house? Something to link her to the murder?"

"I don't know if it links her to the murder but it links her to something. I found a pouch with a roll of money and a small packet with some white powder in it."

"Really? What was in the packet and how much money are we talking about?"

"That I don't know because the Captain walked in and took everything."

"I'd say the white powder was cocaine. That means she's buying and she needs cash. I wonder where Prunella would get money to buy drugs."

"Right and if it was legitimate money, why wasn't it in the bank?"

"This definitely implicates her in something and it doesn't look good, Mabel."

"I guess that's something we'll have to check out, Sheriff Smee."

"Yes, I think we will, Deputy Wickles."

My heart skipped a beat. "You mean I can be a real deputy?"

"Nah, I was just joking." Then, I guess he saw how disappointed I looked because he said, "You can pretend though, Mabel."

I trudged off home, pretending to be thrilled.

Chapter Twenty One

It was almost ten when Flori called. She was all excited about her book club.

"Oh Mabel, I wish you could've been there. It was so much fun. And, guess who came? Erma! She seemed quite preoccupied at first but about half way through she relaxed and really had a ball."

"That's great. I'm glad for Erma, Flori. Did she say anything about Murray? How he's doing?"

It took a minute or two for my friend to remember.

"No, I don't think she said anything. Of course, she was talking mostly with Delores so I couldn't hear what she was saying. It was so much fun, Mabel. You have to come next time. It isn't the same when you're not there."

"Flori, if you were having so much fun without me, why would you need me there? I think it's good for you to do things on your own once in awhile."

Perhaps I should have worded that a bit differently. There was another moment of silence and then, a sob. I waited for the first wave of hysteria to pass.

"Are you finished now, Flori? You know I didn't mean that I wanted to do things on my own, right? I meant that I thought it was nice for you to be able to enjoy an evening with a group of people without me being there. That's all I was saying. I didn't say that I didn't want to be with you."

Another wave of hysteria rolled past.

"Flori, would you stop crying? I'm sorry that I upset you. Could we talk about your evening now? Could we change the subject? Please?"

There were several sniffles and a long nose blow.

"Mabel, you didn't upset me by what you said. I was feeling so awful that you had to spend the evening all alone. You must've been so bored and lonely. I can't believe that I could be so selfish and go off like that, having a good time while you're stuck at home with all those cats."

"My cats aren't all that bad. Don't forget you're stuck at home with Jake every night."

"Oh Mabel, you are so funny." The hysterical tears turned to hysterical laughter, which brought on more tears.

When calmness restored, I said, "Well, I didn't exactly stay at home all the time. I did drop over to visit someone."

"You did?"

"Do I detect a bit of disappointment there, Friend?"

"No, of course not, Mabel. My only concern is what kind of trouble you got yourself into, that's all."

"Flori, you don't have to always think I'm going to get into trouble. Actually, I might even solve the murder case."

There was a long sigh on the other end.

"See, Mabel. I told you, you can't stay out of trouble. That's why I wish you would've been with me at the book club meeting."

"I said I might solve a murder. That doesn't mean I got into trouble."

"What about going over to Prunella's?"

"Well, I thought I should pop over to see how she was doing. There's nothing wrong with that. No one else seems to care about her. Let's face it, Flori, if I hadn't gone over to check on her, she might be dead right now."

"I'm not saying it didn't turn out for the best, Mabel, but let's really face it; you popped over to see if you could find out anything more about Bernie's murder. Admit it, Mabel."

"I think I know what I was doing there and how I saved her life, Flori."

"Okay, but I know you and I know when you're up to something."

"Whatever, Flori. I don't know why you seem to know more about me than I do."

"You're an easy person to read, that's all."

"By the way, I want you to promise that if you or Jake or whomever you send over to my house to check on me, finds me unconscious, please do not let Herman Wheeler practice CPR on me. Will you promise me that, Flori?"

Flori was silent.

"Flori," I said, "I'm not asking for the world. It's just that I don't want Herman Wheeler touching me."

"Oh Mabel, how can I ever leave you to yourself again? One day on your own and you find another dead beaten up body. Murder follows you like sunshine follows the rain. What's going to happen now? It's such a tragedy." She started sniffling.

"No, Flori, before you start to cry – Prunella is not dead. At least, I don't think she is. Maybe I should call the hospital to see how she's doing. In fact, I'll do that right now and get back to you."

Before Flori could discourage me, I said good-bye and hung up.

I waited on 'hold' for several minutes and listened to Elvis before May asked if she could help me. May West, along with Nurse Grappley, are two hospital icons. Grappley is as intimidating as May is approachable. Everyone was certain that when computers came in, Ms. West would retire, but much to everyone's amazement and delight, the eighty-something widow took up the challenge and kept her job. On the other hand, everyone was praying Nurse Grappley would retire and give up but it seems she's sticking it out too.

"May, can you tell me how Prunella is doing?"

"Oh Mabel, I heard you found her in her little house. What a horrible experience for you to endure. How are you, sweetheart?"

"I'm fine. I'm really concerned about Prunella though. Is she conscious? Did they find out who did this to her?"

"I hear she's doing quite well now. She's lucky you came along when you did, Mabel. Such a terrible thing, isn't it? A person never knows how they'll handle stress until it happens to them. And, living alone like that. I'm so happy that my daughter lives close by. Who knows, I might be tempted to take drugs once in awhile too if I got too lonely."

"Drugs? They knew Prunella took drugs?"

"Oops, maybe I wasn't supposed to say anything but since you're the one who found her, I think you should know." She lowered her voice. "Yes, I heard she took some kind of drug and was so dizzy from it, she fell and hit her head. She was also drinking quite a bit lately so it could've been a deadly mixture. Such a sad story."

"Really? She wasn't attacked by anyone?"

"Oh no, she definitely denies that."

"She's conscious then?"

"Yes, she's awake but I'm sure she has a terrible headache."

"Did she say what she hit her head on?"

"I don't know but I overheard someone say that the police didn't find a trace of blood in her house except on her and the bed, of course."

"No, I didn't either. What did she hit her head on? I doubt she'd start to bleed after she got into bed. Wouldn't it spurt all over the place right away? You're sure she didn't say there was an intruder?"

"I'm sure. She insists that she fell and hit her head on something. I doubt she even remembers what it was now."

"Maybe she doesn't remember what really happened to her then either. I'd bet my store that someone hit her, May."

"I think you're right. If I hear anything different, do you want me to let you know?"

"That would be great. I can always pass the information on to Reg too. By the way, he and I are working this case together so we'd appreciate anything you have to offer. If I'm not home, call me at work, okay, May?"

"That's wonderful to hear that you and Sheriff Smee are working together. All I ever see around here are those police officers from the city. What's happened to Jim and Scully? I haven't seen them in ages."

"Well, Reg was at home feeling sorry for himself and I think he sent the boys off to do traffic duty. We'll probably see a spike in parking tickets in the next few days. And, let's hope that it is only 'days' and not any longer."

I could hear noise in the background and May said, "Gotta go, Mabel. I'll talk to you later."

I hung the phone up and it rang ten minutes later.

"Mabel," Flori yelled in my ear before I had time to say a greeting. "What's this about you and Reg working together? You did not tell me about that."

"When did you hear this?"

"You know better than to keep a secret from me."

"Flori, I meant to tell you about Reg and me but we got so preoccupied with Prunella, I forgot. It's no big deal anyway. You know we like solving crimes together."

"First of all, it is a big deal. You were spending time with Reg while his wife was at our book club - which you knew, Mabel. It doesn't look good to see a single woman going to visit a man whose wife is not at home. You never think about things like that before you do them. What will all the neighbors say? Have you thought of that?"

"Flori, you have to stop bawling me out for everything. I did stop in to visit Reg and we sat outside in his lawn chairs discussing the case. Is Beth concerned?"

There was a sniffle. "Of course, Beth isn't concerned. I just worry about you and your reputation, that's all."

"Well, if Beth isn't worried, then don't you be. Who told you I'd been over to Reg's anyway?"

"I don't think you want to know."

Whenever Flori says that, I know who it is.

"How did Esther find out? Does that woman trail me all over the place?"

"Maybe she does. Anyway, she said she saw the two of you sitting outside drinking beer. She made sure to call to tell me. I told her she was a liar because I know that you don't drink beer."

"She was close enough to hear what we were talking about? What was she doing - hiding behind the bushes?"

"She says she just walked past."

"Well, I didn't see her so she obviously was being sneaky. And, how did she hear what we were talking about?"

"I think that came later. She called on her cell phone from the hospital. Did you say something to May about working with Reg?"

"She was at the hospital? Man, I'm going to have to have eyes in the back of my head. I should really go and pay her a visit, the old goat."

"No, don't pay Esther a visit. You know if you do that, it will end up in a big fight and she'll cause you more harm than it's worth."

"You're right, Flori. Well, I'd better go and pay some attention to my family here. If I don't feed them soon, they'll start climbing my drapes. Thanks for letting me know, Flori. I'll talk to you tomorrow."

"Okay, Mabel. Remember that I love you and I always have your best interests at heart."

"I know you do, Mrs. Flanders. Speaking of my heart – when are you going to bring some of those sweet rich cinnamon buns around to the shop again?"

It is so much pleasanter to listen to Flori laughing than yelling or sobbing.

Chapter Twenty Two

Sheriff Smee stopped in about eleven on Tuesday morning. Somehow, he managed to arrange it right when Flori walked in with her cinnamon buns. I won't complain, however, because I was happy to see both of them. The sheriff looked much better than the night before and he had some news for me.

"I visited the hospital early this morning, Mabel, and I think you'll be surprised at what I found out," he said. This he said after finishing one gigantic cinnamon bun and downing his first cup of coffee.

"Really?" I said. "You were up to the hospital? Did you see Prunella?"

"I did. She's trying to say that she was alone and hit her head but she'll have hard time sticking to her story."

"Why's that?"

"Because," he said, with a smug look, "I sent Scully and Jim out last night to check out all the bushes and hedges around Prunella's home and guess what they found about four blocks from Prunella's house?"

This is one irritating factor when trying to solve a murder case with Reg - he insists on making you guess.

"I have no idea. What did they find?"

"Oh, Mabel," Flori said. "Take a guess. I'll say a bloody brick. Am I right?"

"Flori, your eyes are literally sparkling. I don't think you should enjoy this so much."

Reg laughed. "Really, that's a good guess. Imagine if it was another brick. That would make for quite the mystery. Actually, it was a wrought iron frying pan. We took it to the lab at the hospital and they figure it's Prunella's blood all right."

"Why would she lie, Reg? I don't understand."

He shrugged. "I don't know but she might be afraid. Or, maybe she really doesn't remember. She took quite a hit and the alcohol level in her blood was out of this world."

"You're kidding? That much alcohol? And, drugs? I heard she had some in her system too."

He nodded. "You heard about that, did you? Well, they're not sure what type of drug it was. The lab is checking it with the substance that you found. I'm thinking someone maybe put something into her drink. And then, there's that money. It doesn't look good for Prunella."

"Speaking of her drink, did anyone check for fingerprints on the other glass? There was one empty glass that I'm sure was Prunella's but there was another one with some rum left in it. If there are, that will tell us who was visiting."

Reg nodded. "I haven't heard the results yet. Maxymowich sent it away for testing. Let's hope the prints weren't removed."

Flori reached down the front of her muumuu top and pulled out about four tissues. In less than three seconds, she was bawling her eyes out.

"Flori," I said. "Goodness sake, can't you find a better place to keep your tissues? Why are you crying anyway?"

She wiped away some tears from her pink cheeks and sniffed. "Because I don't know what's happening to our lovely little town, that's why. Mabel, people we've known all our lives are killing people we've known all our lives." Another sniff and stifled sob. "And, they're using a brick we might've walked past dozens of times." Just the thought of that seemed to bring on another volley of tears.

"Didn't you cry enough about that already?" I asked. "Instead of crying and carrying on, we have to find out who did this."

"But now," she said. "Now, there are people we've known all our lives, putting drugs into drinks. Not only that, the person drinking those drinks, never drank before." She magically pulled out another handful of tissues with one hand and in her other hand, she gripped the wad of wet soggy used tissues.

"Well," I said. "That's not entirely true."

"What's not entirely true?"

"Prunella might've sort of had a bit of a problem before."

Reg's eyes widened. "Prunella Flowers had a drinking problem? You mean before Bernie's murder?"

"Well, that's what she told me but it was in strictest confidence so I'd appreciate it if you never mentioned it to anyone." I looked at Flori. "Flori?"

"Why are you looking at me? You know I won't say anything to anyone."

"You have a tendency to forget sometimes, that's all. I'm reminding you now."

She sniffed and rolled up all the Kleenex into a ball about the size of a medium cantaloupe. "I won't say anything if you don't, Mabel."

"I'm not saying this to hurt your feelings; it's just that I don't want everyone thinking Prunella is a drunk and a drug addict, that's all."

"I think we've discussed Prunella's drinking habits enough," Reg said. "However, if someone got her drunk, put drugs in her drink and then hit her with a very hard object, I think we'd better realize that this is no kid's game here. We're talking about either one unsavory character or more. This is getting more complicated and I don't want either one of you getting hurt. If you hear something, you come to me. Don't try solving anything on your own. Whoever tried to kill Prunella could just as easily do the same thing to you. You might be the next victim. I mean it."

"And I mean it too, Mabel," Flori piped in. "Don't get involved in this. If it's a big drug ring, the Mafia will be involved and they'll kill you as soon as look at you. Isn't that right, Reg?"

"You said it, Flori."

"Thanks, Reg," I said. "Now Flori will be watching every move I make and worrying day and night."

"I already do anyway, Mabel."

Reg stood up.

"Well, ladies, I'm going to try to see what else I can dig up."

"Does Maxymowich know about the frying pan?" I asked.

Reg nodded. "I can't really keep things like that to myself, Mabel. After all, we do want to find out who killed Bernie and it isn't a contest." He walked to the door but turned and smiled. "Wish I could solve one murder case before I retire though. It would be like icing on the cake."

It would be. It would be icing on my cake too.

+

Chapter Twenty Three

The rest of my day went by quite smoothly. Most people who came in wanted to talk about the murder and about Prunella but some had the decency to buy a thing or two. No one seemed to know much of anything. I made sure to question everyone too. Sometimes the most innocent remark could lead to a clue or even solving a case.

Most of them were very concerned about Murray McFerguson. He was sinking deeper and deeper into depression and Erma didn't know what to do. I hadn't heard from her so I supposed she didn't know anymore about Bernie and Melanie. No one talked much about Melanie. She was apparently hiding out in her parent's home and not seeing anyone. It struck me that it could be house arrest because obviously she would not be an escape risk. It sounded like the city cops had interviewed all of her neighbors and almost everyone in Parson's Cove, for that matter. Flori said Jake told her that they talked to all the men who met at Main Street Café. Obviously, someone knew something.

My Tuesday went by smoothly but I knew Wednesday wouldn't be quite as pleasant. Delores came to the shop at eight that morning and I walked over to Flori's so we could go together to the Nursing Home. She still didn't totally trust me.

"Flori," I said. "What kind of person do you think I am? You really think I would leave you all alone with Calvin and all these elderly people?"

She took much too long to answer.

As usual everyone was waiting for us. At least this time the weather was cooperating. Smiling faces, walkers, and canes filled the front sidewalk. Some were sitting in their wheelchairs watching and wishing they could go. A few just sat and stared, having no idea what was going on. They were probably the happiest.

Everyone, including the ones who were staring, let out a loud cheer when they saw us coming down the sidewalk. As we got closer we noticed most of them were laughing and pointing. I looked at Flori and she looked at me.

"What's with them?" I asked. "I think we're more to be pitied than laughed at, don't you?"

Flori turned a pretty pink, which seemed to enhance the bright pink empire waist top she was wearing. "Do you think my slip is showing?" she said. "I'll walk ahead and you check, Mabel."

"It's not your slip. They're pointing at something. Not us." I turned around and there walking as proud as could be was Sammy, my one and only white cat.

"Sammy, what are you doing here? You bad cat." I reached down and picked him up. He proceeded to purr and act as if he'd won the Nobel Prize for best behaved cat.

Flori started laughing. "Mabel, you should take him over for those folks to see him. I bet they would love to pet him. Some homes bring animals in for the residents, you know. I think Sammy would be a really good cat for that." She reached over and scratched the cat behind his ears. The cat reacted swiftly by scrambling out of my arms and into Flori's. Thus, letting everyone know how love deprived he was.

Calvin sat in the bus with the door open, scowling as we walked up. His face was enough to ruin anyone's day. Flori proudly showed Sammy around and after each pet and snuggle, I would lead that person onto the bus.

"Say 'good morning' to our happy driver, Mr. Koots," I said to each one that I brought up the steps and past the driver's seat. Mr. Koots replied to each with a grunt. Somehow not one elderly person took offense.

We were finally all settled in. It should've been Calvin's job to walk down the aisle to count and check each occupant but Flori very willingly did that. It took awhile because she had to stop and hug each one. I was getting almost as restless as the driver was. To say that he was getting restless was putting it mildly. He started the motor, tapped his foot, and every few seconds would turn around and ask Flori how much longer she was going to take.

"We don't have all day here, you know, Mrs. Flanders," he said. "Some of us want to get back home before dark."

That set the old folks in a commotion because they didn't want to drive home in the dark either. At least, not the adventurous ones. Of course, some like Mary Jane Smith couldn't hear anything anyway. She took her seat beside me again.

"Don't forget," she whispered. "Watch Calvin's feet when he comes back."

I nodded. At least this part of the trip was fun for me. I have to say that even after all these years, it still felt strange sitting beside my old teacher and have her whispering in my ear.

We were almost into the city when a few in the back rows started laughing and squealing. Everyone looked back and down the aisle. There, walking as if he owned the bus, strolled Sammy. He looked up at each occupant and when he spied me, he raced over and jumped on my lap. Of course, now that he knew he'd been a bad cat, he would snuggle and purr. It was all to the delight of the passengers. I'd never seen them so cheerful. Perhaps Flori was right. It might be a good idea to rent him out to the nursing home. The thought of rent money did cross my mind for a second but if Flori knew that, she'd be devastated.

The only one who wasn't impressed was Calvin Koots. However, I doubted anything would impress him.

"Mabel," he yelled. "Get that cat off the bus."

I looked out the window. We were doing seventy miles an hour on the freeway.

"How do you propose I do that, Calvin?" I yelled back.

"I don't care how you do it. I don't want that cat on my bus."

Suddenly the busload of seniors came to life. Everyone started shouting at once. If I hadn't stood up and told them to shut up and sit down, I think Calvin might have been injured. Not that it would bother me too much but throwing things like books at someone who's driving a fast moving vehicle isn't too wise.

"Don't worry," I told them. "We won't throw Sammy off the moving bus." I turned to Calvin. "And, Calvin, you don't have to worry because I'll look after the cat while we're at the mall."

He didn't say anything after that and the rest of the drive was quiet. Sammy moved over to Miss MJ's lap and sat there until we arrived.

After unloading us and grumbling about how long it was taking Calvin took off, screeching the school bus wheels. I never even knew you could do that. He was obviously in a rush to go somewhere.

MJ was watching the bus too. "See, Mabel," she said. "That man is up to something."

"I don't understand why he's the one taking you to the city anyway. Whatever happened to Bill Williams? Why'd he quit?"

Miss MJ shrugged. "I don't know but I sure wish he'd come back. Maybe it was getting too hard for him, driving the school kids and then us too. I'm sure we're harder to handle."

"I'm going to talk to Flori again and see if she can't get Jake to do something. She was going to but probably forgot."

"We'd be eternally grateful." She'd been holding Sammy while I helped Flori getting people off the bus and now she handed him back. Sammy looked at me with a very smug look on his face. Well, we'd see how smug that look would be when I bought a collar and leash for him.

To my surprise, my cat took to a collar and leash like Reg to cinnamon buns. Of course, he was getting the attention of every shopper. It was a good thing that he was so well behaved because the security guard came around twice to check us out. The second time, Sammy was sitting in the cart as if he owned it. We did discover, however, that the restaurant wouldn't let us in so we bought some food at the food court and found a bench. MJ stayed with me this time. I don't think it was my company but Sammy's that drew her.

This time again, Calvin was late. Ten minutes. Once again, we had to coax him to help. He mumbled and grumbled but finally agreed to put some packages in the compartments on the outside of the bus.

"Look," MJ whispered in my ear. "See how he's walking?"

Sure as anything, the bus driver walked as if he had blisters on the bottom of his feet.

"When we get back to the Home, I'll ask him what's wrong with his feet." I told her.

She nodded and grinned. "Best not to get him upset before we get home."

Sammy sat on my lap and since he was being so good, I removed the collar and leash. Before I could stop him, he was down on the floor and up by the driver's seat. Fortunately, Calvin didn't notice. Flori was calling my name from a seat close to the back of the bus.

"Mabel," she said. She started waving her hands and arms and pointing towards Calvin. Then, she whispered very loudly, "Get that cat out of there."

"I know." It was easier said than done. I called Sammy but not too loudly because I didn't want Calvin to hear me and I didn't want him to see the cat. If I snuck up to the front and startled the driver, who knew where we would end up? We'd turned onto the freeway now and there were four lanes of traffic travelling from fifty to eighty miles an hour.

Sammy was so preoccupied with Calvin's shoe that there was no way I could get his attention. If Calvin looked down he couldn't miss seeing a white cat sitting there sniffing his boot. Twice Calvin lifted his foot off the gas and stepped on the brake. I held my breath as Sammy followed his foot from the gas pedal to the brake. Fortunately, traffic was heavy and Calvin didn't dare take his eyes off the road. Perhaps, if he didn't notice Sammy, he wouldn't notice me grabbing Sammy. Perhaps.

The bus became very quiet as everyone watched me lower myself to the floor and crawl on hands and knees to the front of the bus. I crouched down behind the driver's seat and waited. Sammy took his nose off the shoe for a moment to look at me. I have no idea what he was thinking but he quickly went back to sniffing Calvin's size twelve shoes. What, on earth could Calvin have stepped in that made my cat so attracted to the bottom of his boot? Calvin, I noticed, was watching the traffic coming up on the left. There were several semi trailers trying to get by. It was now or never. I reached out, grabbed Sammy, and scrambled backwards to my seat. The busload of seniors burst into cheers and clapping. Calvin looked back and gave all of us a dirty look. By this time, I was safely back in my seat, trying to hang onto my cat. He definitely wanted to get back to smelling the driver's clunky brown work boots.

The only way I could keep that fanatical cat from jumping off my lap was to put the leash back on. I held him tight all the way back to Parson's Cove. As soon as the bus rolled to a stop in front of Parson's Cove Restful Retirement Retreat, I loosened my grip on Sammy's leash. He bolted off my lap and ran up to Calvin's shoes, sniffing and pawing.

"Get that dang cat away from me," Calvin yelled as he kicked at the cat with his steel-toed boots.

Never kick an animal in front of anyone over seventy.

"What's the matter with you?" one old woman screamed as she hit Calvin over the head with her purse. "How would you like it if I kicked you?"

With that, a chorus of protests went up and Calvin actually looked at me for help.

"You should be ashamed," I said and grabbed Sammy. "What have you got on your shoes anyway that drives my cat crazy?"

"Nothing. You can look. I don't have anything on my shoes. You've got one crazy cat, that's all and you make sure he never comes on this bus again or I'm going to report you, Mabel."

"Don't worry, I will never be coming on this bus again and if I have anything to do with it, you won't either, Calvin Koots. You are the last person who should be put in charge of elderly people. I hope someday when you're old and decrepit that you get treated just like you treated these people."

"You tell him, Mabel," Sam Dudley said when he walked by, making sure to give me a little pat where he shouldn't have. Thankfully, Flori was right behind him and gave him a good slap on his arm.

I let Sammy down and he went right for Calvin's feet again. Before Calvin could kick, I yanked on the leash and pulled a very uncooperative cat out of the bus. Calvin shut the door and away went the little yellow school bus down the road.

As soon as Mr. Kinney walked out the door, the returning travelers surrounded him. Everyone was talking at once and everyone talked about Mr. Koots kicking the cat. The bewildered manager couldn't make any sense of it until someone pointed to me – me and my cat.

Flori (because she insisted on accompanying me) and I spent the next ten minutes in the manager's office trying to explain what happened. Sammy sat on my lap and gave himself a sponge bath with his tongue and paws. When he got a little too carried away, I pulled his leg down and held it. Flori did most of the talking and by the time we left, she'd convinced him that Calvin should not drive the bus anymore. When Mr. Kinney opened the door, four people almost fell into the room. A couple of them were too deaf to hear anything but when the other two started to cheer, they clapped their hands.

Koot's days were kaput.

In a manner of speaking, so were mine. I told Flori my decision as we walked home. I waited for the tears and pleading but none came.

"Mabel," she said. "Even when Calvin is gone, I don't think I could do another trip with you anyway."

"With me?"

She nodded. "You are a terrible shopper and it seems that when you're around, there's always some kind of trouble. You have a way of getting all those old people in an uproar. My nerves can't take it anymore. No, they'll have to find someone to replace you."

"Replace me?"

She nodded. "I'm sorry, sweetie. You know I love you to pieces but there are some things you shouldn't do and one is go to the city with elderly people."

As I said, my days were also kaput and I was very happy about that.

Chapter Twenty Four

Thursday morning was hot again. There was no breeze and not a cloud in the sky. My window air conditioner at my shop droned on, nonstop. I pulled down the blinds in my front windows and trusted that everyone would realize I was open and trying to stay as cool as I could. Even in the heat, however, I still brewed some coffee and kept a supply of muffins in my little fridge in the back room. Not that I did it for Captain Maxymowich exactly but in case he did happen to drop by, I would be prepared.

Flori came over about ten and we had coffee in front of the a/c unit. She left early because she says that she sweats like a pig when it's so hot. I have no idea about pigs' sweat but I took her word for it so didn't argue. Ten minutes after she left, Reg arrived.

"Boy, it's a hot one today, Mabel. How about a cup of coffee?" He took off his cap. There was a rim of sweat all around it.

"You wear a cap on such a hot day?"

"It keeps the sun out of my eyes."

"And you want a cup of coffee?"

"Not if you've got a nice cold beer in your fridge."

"Well, sorry about that. You sure you want coffee on such a hot day?"

"Not unless you have cold beer in your fridge."

"All right, I get the picture. Sit down in front of the air conditioner and I'll pour you a cup of coffee. I'll grab you a muffin too if you like."

Reg was sitting in the wicker chair, his eyes closed with his face to the wind. He didn't even hear me. I fixed his coffee and buttered some muffins for him. He looked grateful when I handed it to him. Since there's no point in talking while he's eating, I waited patiently. Mutt, my neighbor from the hardware store next door, popped in and grabbed a coffee.

"You're drinking coffee on a hot day like this too?" I said.

He glanced over at Reg who didn't even notice Mutt. On the other hand, perhaps he didn't want to speak with his mouth full.

"Just an excuse to come in, Mabel. Have you heard anything more about Prunella? I hear she's really into drugs and booze now. You always think it's the kids who are foolish." He took a swallow. "Just goes to show that older ones can get hooked on them too."

"Mutt, we don't know if she was hooked on drugs. Someone could've put something in her drink, you know. Don't jump to conclusions."

"You say someone slipped something into her drink? Oh man, that's awful. Do you think the same person who killed Bernie, tried to murder Prunella?"

"I don't know. If it is, then there's only one killer out there."

His eyes widened. "You're right. If it's someone different, that means there are two killers at large. I don't know about you but I make sure my house is locked up at night. The wife and I were thinking of investing in a guard dog too. Course, one dog was already killed so don't know if it's worth it." He glanced over at the sheriff who was now on his third muffin. "Doesn't seem Reg is getting too stressed-out about it, does it?"

I lowered my voice, although I was sure Reg couldn't hear over the noise anyway, "Don't worry,

Mutt, I'm sure Captain Maxymowich is on top of everything."

He nodded. "I suppose. Actually, there's quite a few of us who wish Sheriff Smee could find the killer. Be nice just to show that Parson's Cove has a real police force too. Know what I mean, Mabel?"

It was my turn to nod. "Well, don't give up on us. Reg and I are checking a few things out, too."

He drained his cup and handed it to me. "Atta girl, Mabel. We were hoping you could help out." He patted my arm and left the building.

Before I could wash out Mutt's cup, Reg handed me his for a refill. I was going to have to start setting a few rules about coffee mugs. My only problem with making the men wash their cups is that I have to wash them over again most of the time anyway. I've noticed too that they don't have much respect for tea towels. After they finish with the washing and drying, I usually find the towel all bunched up in a ball and stuck on some shelf.

I handed Reg his fresh coffee and was about to say something about not being anyone's slave when I glanced down and saw his brown leather sandals.

"Reg," I said. "Are you supposed to be wearing sandals? Aren't police officers required to wear boots? I've never seen you in sandals before. What if you had to run after a crook?"

"If I had to run after a crook, I'd hope to be wearing sneakers." He reluctantly pulled himself off the chair. "I'd also hope to be ten years younger and twenty pounds lighter."

I laughed. "Well, there's no way you can turn the clock back. So, if you don't plan on chasing any crooks, what are you going to do today? We have a mystery to solve still and it seems the people of Parson's Cove are counting on us."

"Actually, Mabel, I was thinking that I could sneak back into my office and discreetly question the Captain to see how the case is going." He sighed. "If I find anything out, I'll get back to you."

He was standing with his hand on the doorknob when I realized how our sheriff must look to those city cops. To us, he was just Reg. He'd been our sheriff now for umpteen years and although he wasn't a super hero, he got things done in his own slow and easy way. His sweaty cap was pulled down over his forehead, his light blue uniform shirt was open at the neck and his sleeves were rolled up. I guess his gun with all the paraphernalia that goes with it made him too hot because he wasn't wearing it. There were some slight perspiration marks under his arms and between his shoulder blades. His dark navy pants were probably a size too small now and there was a bit too much ankle showing above his sandals.

His sandals. Shoes. Boots. Feet.

Something suddenly clicked in my brain.

"Reg," I said. "Let me know if you hear something. I've got an important phone call to make now." I hurried over, removed his hand from the knob and opened the door. "I'm sorry to rush you out but I don't want any of the heat coming in either."

He looked a little stunned but since he's used to my sudden personality changes, he didn't protest. I glanced out the window and saw that he could run quite fast in his sandals to get into his air-conditioned patrol car.

I picked up the phone and called Flori.

"Flori, remember when we went to the city with the seniors?"

"You mean, yesterday? I'm not quite that forgetful yet."

"I'm not really asking if you remember if we went, I'm just starting my conversation that way."

"All right. What about our trip to the city? Please, don't tell me that you really want to come again, Mabel. I know I hurt your feelings but I think it's for the best if I get someone else. And, since I've already asked someone and she's said yes, I can't make any changes now. I'm so sorry. I know I should never have said all those terrible things to you. Can you ever forgive me, Mabel?"

With that, she began to cry. I waited for a minute or so because there was no way she could hear anything I was saying. When there was a lull after she blew her nose, I said, "There is nothing to forgive, Flori. You didn't say any horrible things to me and I think it's wonderful that you've found someone to take my place."

More sniffles. "Do you mean that? You don't really mind that I've asked someone else? You realize that this person does not 'take your place,' right? There is no one who could ever take your place, Mabel."

"I know. What I'm wondering about is if Calvin Koots wore the same shoes all day yesterday."

"Pardon me?"

"I know this sounds weird but can you remember, Flori? Did Calvin have the same shoes on for the whole trip or was he wearing different shoes on the way home?"

"My goodness, Mabel, I don't know what kind of shoes Calvin was wearing. The only reason I know he was wearing those heavy Army boots is because your cat was trying to tear them off his feet. Did you ever find out why? You have to admit that Sammy was acting very strange."

"He was and Sammy is not a strange cat. He's one of my sanest ones. There was something on the outside or else on the inside of those shoes that drove Sammy crazy. Remember Miss MJ saying how Calvin walked differently when it was time to go home?"

"I don't know; maybe he stepped in something. What difference does it make anyway, Mabel?"

"I'm not sure but I'd like to find out. Isn't it just driving you crazy not knowing?"

Flori sighed, dramatically. "Why would something that I don't know anything about and that I have no interest in finding out, drive me crazy?"

"I guess I see your point. I think I'll give Miss MJ a call and see if she remembers. By the way, who is taking my place for the next trip to the city?"

Another sigh. "Not taking your place, Mabel. I thought I'd ask Erma because it will give her a break from Murray. Jake said he hasn't started coming back to the restaurant yet. Remember how he would always walk over with Biscuit and he'd have coffee with the guys? Murray, that is, not Biscuit." She sniffed. "It's so sad, isn't it? I always wonder how you'll make out when your cats start to leave you."

"Flori, my cats won't be leaving me soon and when they do, I'll manage just fine. Besides, since they have nine lives and I have only one, I'm sure I'll be leaving them first. You'd better start planning what to do with them because in my Will, I've left them all to you."

She must've thought I was joking because she was laughing hysterically when I hung up.

It took several minutes for someone to track down my old English teacher but as I waited, the different sounds from the retirement home entertained me. I realize that old age and senility are nothing to joke about but I certainly hope that someone will gently place a pillow over my face when I don't know who I am anymore. And, I'm not joking.

"Mabel?" MJ said, with a slightly out of breath wheeze. "Is that you?"

"Yes, MJ, it's me."

"Or, do you mean, 'it is I?'"

"Yes, it is I, Mabel Wickles."

"Oh Mabel, you're a hoot. I almost wish I was back teaching school again. You have no idea how much joy it was to teach you."

"Were."

"Were what?"

"Almost wish you *were* back teaching school. Remember, if you are expressing some form of wish, desire, or uncertainty, use the specific verb form that reflects the mood of uncertainty."

When MJ had finished laughing, she said, "Now you know why you brought such joy to my heart."

"Really? I think you're the first person who's ever said that I brought them joy. I think I shower most people with things like headaches."

"See? You have a wonderful sense of humor. You kept the class in an uproar. Well, until you were expelled, that is."

"Yes, we have some wonderful memories. Now, speaking of memories – can you remember if Calvin was wearing the same shoes all day yesterday?"

"Oh no, he never wears the same shoes. He has sneakers on for the drive there and then coming home, he has those awful big brown boots. I guess that's why he walks so funny. It never made much sense to me but I did get a kick out of watching him in those boots. Are you wondering why he changed shoes, Mabel?"

"Yes, I am. Aren't you?"

"Well, I wasn't before but I guess I am now. How will you find out? Are you going to ask him?"

"Are you kidding? He thinks that I took away his job so he won't answer any questions from me, that's for sure."

"What will you do?"

"I'll just ask around. I'll let you know when I find something out. How does that sound?"

"That sounds wonderful. By the way, I heard you won't be coming with us on our day trip anymore. I'll miss you, Mabel."

"I know you'll miss me, MJ, but probably not as much as Sam Dudley will."

MJ was still chuckling when I hung up.

Chapter Twenty Five

It was so hot by noon that the inside knob of the door was perspiring. I wanted to check on Charlie Thompson but I dreaded going outside almost as much as I did in the winter when it was thirty below zero. This time instead of piling on sweaters and coats, I grabbed sunglasses. The cotton shirt I was wearing already had long sleeves so it protected me somewhat from the sun's deadly rays. Since I look outlandish in a hat, I decided I would walk as fast as I could and hope I didn't get sunstroke.

I turned the 'open' sign around to 'closed' and didn't fill in the 'Be back in ... minutes' part (which I never do because the only person who would know when you're coming back would be the one who saw you put the sign up). There wasn't one person on the street. I headed over to the north side so I could be in the shade. Charlie sat in his usual spot – the bench in front of the library. He was wearing his red and black plaid flannel shirt with his denim overalls. At least, he'd put on an old straw hat that protected his face from the sun.

"Hi Charlie," I said. "It's a really hot day, isn't it?"

He shrugged. "I like it. Why don't you, Mabel?"

"Oh well, I like it; it's just that it's a bit too warm for me."

"You complain when it's cold too."

I laughed. "Charlie, you told a good joke. Did you know that?"

It was hard to tell but I think a faint smile passed his lips.

"Did you want to know something, Mabel?"

I hate to think that Charlie feels the only reason that I talk to him is to get information so I said, "No, I thought I'd just sit and visit for awhile."

"Now you're telling the joke, right?"

I looked over at him. I swear there was a twinkle in his eye.

"Well," I said. "I suppose we could do both. Isn't that what visiting is? I'll tell you some of the interesting things that I know and you can tell me what you know."

He was beginning to rock slowly back and forth. I had to move fast.

"Have you seen any strange sights in the night, Charlie?"

He stopped. "There are always strange sights," he said. "You aren't going to the city with Flori anymore?"

"Boy, word sure gets around, doesn't it? No, Erma is going in my place. I really can't afford to take a day away from my store anyway." We sat in silence for several minutes. "By the way, do you know anything about the shoes that Calvin Koots wears?"

Now, anyone else would have some sort of reaction to a strange question like that. Not Charlie.

"I don't know about his shoes but I know where he goes all the time."

"You mean to Scooter's? Or, does he go other places in the night too?"

"He goes other places. Sometimes I see him running around in the night."

"Running around? Where, Charlie?"

"To a house. To the car wash."

"He goes to the car wash? You mean he washes his car in the night?"

Charlie, however, had shut down. This was probably the most he'd said to me in the past year so I knew I should count it as a privilege and be thankful.

I sat beside him for several more minutes so he'd know that I appreciated his company and didn't come only for information. The information he'd given me made me curious though. Where was Calvin going in the night? Which house? Why was he washing his car at night? Too bad that Bernie was killed in the daytime. On the other hand, where was Calvin the afternoon that Bernie was murdered? Is that what Charlie meant? Calvin was behind the carwash when Bernie was murdered?

Chapter Twenty Six

There must've been some sort of cold front that went through during the night because about three in the morning, thunder boomed and lightning flashed. In fact, the thunder was so loud, I'm sure my bed vibrated an inch or so off the floor. The noise, however, wasn't what woke me up. I woke up in a panic because seven cats were jumping on my bed, meowing and pawing at my face. In many ways, this is reassuring to me because if my house were on fire, those cats would make certain I got out alive.

By the time I settled them down, I was completely awake so I decided to go downstairs and have a drink of water. I'd taken to sleeping in my bed again even though my air conditioner didn't work. Sleeping downstairs with the cats creeping around all night was worse than sleeping in a sweaty nightgown.

I didn't turn any lights on because there was enough light from the outside sky to help me find my way. Three cats followed me. The rest were curled up on my bed. The three who came downstairs chatted all the way down.

"No," I said to them. "I am not getting food for you. I'm getting a drink of water. If you think I'm going to start feeding you in the middle of the night, you're sadly mistaken."

I stood at the kitchen sink and drank my water. People from the city were renting the house behind mine. The old house was empty most of the year and the owner lived in the city. I'd talked to the young man who was renting. I believe he said his name was Jeff and he was staying until September. He seemed pleasant enough. His wife, apparently, would be joining him but she didn't start her vacation until next week. I was surprised to see lights on in the kitchen but then again if I were a normal person, I would have lights on in my kitchen too. Most people don't walk around in the dark. I'm sure the thunder must've jolted him to life too.

I rinsed the glass out and was just about to turn away when I saw the backdoor open and someone coming out. By now, the rain had started and whoever it was had his jacket pulled over his head. Right then there was a flash of lightning but he was moving too fast and I couldn't see his face. I was quite sure it was a man though. The kitchen light remained on so I assumed that Jeff had company. Probably another fisherman, telling tall tales and drinking beer.

The Krueger house behind me has become quite notorious over the past few years. First, there was a murder and then, about a year ago last winter, thieves used it as a storage place for stolen antiques. I guess an empty house is an invitation for crooks, especially when it's secluded. I am the only one who can see if anything is going on there. There are high hedges on both sides of the yard and no houses across from it.

Mr. Krueger and my father were friends many years ago. Well, they were friends as long as both their gardens did well. If either man had a crop failure, they were not on speaking terms. If Mr. Krueger's tomatoes were bigger or redder than my father's were, my father went to bed for a week. Mrs. Krueger was the town gossip but my mother was probably the most cantankerous woman in Parson's Cove so you can imagine their relationship. As soon as Linda Krueger finished school, she moved away from Parson's Cove and after her parents died, she decided to rent the house instead of selling it. For one thing, no one would ever buy it but in the summer, we do have quite a few tourists in town. Our lake is teeming with fish and there are a few nice beaches. If it weren't for the tourists, I would be bankrupt. Not that I get many customers during the week but on the weekend, the place is buzzing.

I listened to the rain pattering on the roof, the thunder rumbling somewhere in the distance and the purr of seven cats. It didn't take long to drift back to sleep. When I awoke, the sky was gray and the wind was howling around the corners of the house.

Flori came into the shop the moment that I unlocked the front door. She carried a large brown bag with a few spots of grease showing here and there.

"Did you hear the latest?" she said, as she plunked the bag down on the counter.

"I don't think so. What's it about?"

"Calvin Koots is suing the Retirement Home."

"What? Why?"

"Because they told him he can't take the bus to the city again. Well, Mr. Kinney didn't but the board members want him out."

"Well, that's just plain crazy. It's obvious that he hates being a senior-sitter and they sure can't stand him. Did he have a contract?"

"Apparently but Jake says there's a probation period so he doesn't stand a chance of winning."

"Is he so poor that he can't make the payments on his taxi?"

"Jake says he's always throwing money around like it's going out of style. He likes to brag and pay for everyone's coffee at the café so he can't be all that broke."

"Charlie says Calvin does a lot of running around during the night. I wonder what he's up to, Flori."

"I don't know, Mabel, but I do know one thing – it's none of our business. Right?"

When she said 'right?' she looked me square in the eye.

"In other words," I said. "You don't want me running around in the middle of the night following Calvin Koots. Right?"

"Right. Now, can we have some coffee? You don't even have it on yet."

"I'm behind this morning. That storm woke me up last night. Or, the cats did. I'm not sure which is to blame but I did lose some sleep. By the way, remember I told you that there was a young fellow renting Krueger's house? Well, he had company last night and they didn't leave until after three. I sure hope that when his wife comes they don't have wild parties all night long."

Flori shook her head. "I'm so glad we don't live by one of those rental houses. In fact, I'll be glad when all these tourists pack up and go home."

"Don't say that. If it weren't for them, I'd be eating at the soup kitchen and sleeping on a park bench."

"Oh Mabel, you know I'd never let you sleep on a park bench." She proceeded to hug the stuffing out of me. When I started to gasp for breath, she squeezed a little harder and said, "And, I mean it about not following Calvin Koots in the dark."

About four, several customers came into the store. All of them were tourists and although they were interested in some of the souvenirs, they seemed more curious about the murder.

An elderly couple dressed as though they were on an African safari, was the first to broach the subject.

"We hear you had a terrible murder here several days ago," the lady said. "Isn't it shocking when such crimes infiltrate small towns? We've never been here before but we read about Mr. Bernstein in the papers and we thought we'd check it out. Do they have any suspects yet?"

"No," I replied. "However, we're making sure our doors are locked and some are getting guard dogs. I hear there are a lot of unsavory characters running around in the streets at night."

Their eyes bulged. "You know this? Why doesn't the sheriff do something about it?"

I glanced around the room and lowered my voice, "Well, between you and me, the sheriff isn't as young as he used to be. He's ready to retire and in my opinion, is just counting the days until he gets his pension."

They both gasped. "That's terrible," the old man said. "Your lives could be in danger."

"Have any tourists been attacked?" she asked.

"Not yet," I said. "And, I'll tell you, it's not good for business. I might have to declare bankruptcy if I don't start selling something. When everyone is living in fear, they don't want to spend much money. My only consolation is that we have a really good soup kitchen in town for the down-and-outers."

The two walked away whispering as they walked down each aisle.

"Thank you, Mr. and Mrs. Langside," I said as I accepted their credit card about ten minutes later. "That will be $87.59."

Mrs. Langside reached over and patted my arm. "I hope everything works out for you, my dear. We mentioned your predicament to your other customers and they've agreed to help you out. Unfortunately, we've decided we won't spend the weekend in Parson's Cove after all, but perhaps we'll return some other time." She gave me a knowing look. "You know, when it's safer. It is a lovely little place and I hope the sheriff will change his ways and get down to solving this crime. Thank you again."

The next three customers all purchased something and when it was time to close shop and I'd chased Esther Flynn out, I added up my sales. I made more in the past hour than I had for the whole week. And, lucky for me, none of the tourists planned to stay in Parson's Cove for the weekend. It was good for my business but the hotel would probably suffer.

"However," as I explained to Reg later on that evening on the phone "it's much easier to solve a murder when the town isn't brimming with nosy tourists."

Chapter Twenty Seven

"Did you find out anything from Maxymowich?" I asked after I'd explained my little plan for getting rid of visitors. As you can well imagine, I did describe things somewhat differently to Reg. For example, I believe I inserted Captain Maxymowich's name for Reg's name. I know how Flori feels about my lying but sometimes it seems to be a necessity. Especially when trying to find a killer. A lie seems like such a lesser sin.

"Not much. He was very careful with his words. I think there's more going on than meets the eye, Mabel. I know they're trying to find whoever murdered Bernie but somehow, they seem to be concentrating on other things too."

"Concentrating on other things? Like what?"

"Like very discreetly asking questions about Scooter Macalvey."

"Really? Do you know what, Reg? Charlie was talking to me about Scooter. He said Calvin Koots goes there at night. I don't trust Calvin one bit. We should try to find out what those two are up to."

There was a moment of silence.

"Reg?"

"I think I was told not to get involved."

"What do you mean, you were told not to get involved? Who told you that?"

"Well, Maxymowich suggested that I concentrate on keeping Parson's Cove safe by doing more patrolling and watching out for the tourists."

"So that's good, Reg. Why don't you patrol in the night and keep your eye on Scooter's house?"

"I believe he distinctly mentioned 'day' patrol. Me and the boys. The big city boys are protecting us by night."

"Oh posh. I'm going to have another talk with Charlie. He'll know what's going on at night and I know one thing, he won't say anything to the Captain unless I tell him to. Even then, he probably wouldn't."

"I don't know, Mabel. You don't want anyone seeing you talking too much to Charlie. We don't want anything happening to him. Besides, Maxymowich will know if Charlie starts snooping around that you're the one behind it."

"I'll be very subtle about it all, don't worry."

Reg snorted. "Mabel, you have no idea what the word, subtle, means. By the way, the Captain called me today before I went over."

"You're kidding. What did he want? Some of your input?"

"No, he wanted the brick back. I guess they're collecting all the evidence and they didn't need me to hold onto it anymore." He sighed. "Guess my usefulness is finished."

"Oh for Pete's sake, Reg, get a grip. You have to stop feeling sorry for yourself. Have you visited Melanie lately?"

"No, I haven't visited anyone. What's the point? I don't know what more I can learn from her."

"Well, I don't know either but we can't just give up. You go and visit her tomorrow because they'll let you in. I'll be stuck at the store all day. At noon, I'll walk over and talk to Charlie again."

"I don't know, Mabel."

"I know, Reg. We can sit on our butts and not do anything or we can try. Someone in Parson's Cove is a murderer and we have to find that person. We have no choice. Now, let's do it."

"If you ever want to go into another line of work, Mabel, you could always be a motivational speaker."

I was glad to hear the chuckle in Reg's voice. I'm sure I have no idea how these wives keep their husbands motivated to do anything.

It was ten before it was completely dark outside. The clouds had rolled away during the day and it was a clear warm night. It was a quarter moon - not too light out and yet not so dark I couldn't see where I was going. At least, in the areas where there were no street lamps.

Maybe Reg had his orders but no one had ordered me to stay inside after nine p.m. and as long as I called Flori before I left, I knew she wouldn't call back. Especially since I told her I was going to try to get a good night's sleep after the awful one I'd had the night before.

"Mabel, don't worry. I won't call and I suggest you take your phone off the hook. You need your sleep because you'll have a shopful of tourists tomorrow. Jake said the town is buzzing with them. They all want to see where Bernie was murdered. I think it's disgusting, don't you?"

"I do but you know human nature. Everyone is intrigued by a mystery."

"I know all too well. I'm glad you aren't sticking your nose into this one, Mabel." Before she hung up, she suggested that I try some warm milk with a bit of cinnamon in it before hitting the sack. I told her that I'd give it a try.

I'd promised Reg that I would talk to Charlie the next afternoon but now that I was outside, I thought I might as well take care of that right way. As my father would say, why put off for tomorrow what you can do today.

I didn't want to give anyone the impression that I was sneaking around; however, I did wear my black jeans with a black long sleeved shirt and black sandals. The only other shoes I owned were sneakers and they were so white they almost glowed in the dark.

Charlie was sitting in his usual spot. He wasn't wearing his straw hat but everything else was the same.

"Hi, Charlie," I said and plopped down beside him. "Are you ready for some adventure?"

I'd never tried this angle with him but it was worth a try.

"What kind of adventure, Mabel?"

"Well, you said that Calvin Koots visits Scooter Macalvey at night. I thought that maybe you and I could check it out. You know, very inconspicuously."

"Someone else might be there."

"Someone else at Scooter's?"

He shook his head. "Someone else is checking them out, inconspicuously."

I tried to control myself but somehow that really tickled my funny bone.

"Why is that so funny, Mabel?"

I couldn't tell him that he sounded like Porky Pig when he said 'inconspicuously,' so I lied and said, "Nothing's funny, Charlie. I'm just excited to think someone else is watching the house too. That's all." I could feel my nose growing but Charlie didn't notice. "Are the city cops keeping an eye on Scooter's garage? Is that what you're saying?"

He nodded.

"So, is there any good hiding place where you and I could watch and no one else could see us?"

He nodded.

"That's good. Could we go there right now?"

Wrong move. Charlie doesn't go anywhere 'right now' and I should've known that.

He started slowly rocking back and forth.

"You're not ready to show me the place yet, is that it?" I asked.

I'll never know if he was ready to show me or not because that was all I was getting out of him for one night. After watching him moving back and forth and humming for several minutes, I decided I'd start off on my own. How hard can it be to find a hiding place for one very small person?

Scooter's garage was facing the back lane so I headed for that lane. Scooter's wife was probably at work so I wouldn't have to worry about running into her. It seemed to me she'd been working the night shift at the hospital for years.

To make my little excursion easier for you to comprehend, you have to realize that many years ago in the old part of Parson's Cove, almost everyone built their garages facing the back lane. My street is the one exception. For some reason I have no back lane and my garage is at the back of my lot facing the street. Any way you look at it, if there's six feet of snow in the winter, there's lots of shoveling to do.

Only the light of the moon illuminated the lane so in other words, it was very dark and in some areas I could hardly see my hand in front of me. Twice I walked into a garbage can but fortunately, I was still quite a ways from Scooter's place. When I was two houses away I stepped into a backyard and listened. It wasn't late yet but the street was very quiet. Of course, there were no young children on this street at all so probably everyone went to bed before ten. Which is where I should have been.

I slowly stepped forward, placing one foot carefully in front of the other, until I was one garage away from Scooter's place. I stopped and listened again. This time, I could hear muffled talking and something making a clanging sound. If I stayed on this side of the lane I wouldn't be able to see into the garage unless I peeked around the corner of the door. Not a good idea. So, I backtracked several homes and slunk across the narrow graveled lane. Now I would be able to look right into Scooter's garage if he opened the door, hopefully some time before the sun came up.

I decided that instead of trying to sneak across in front of each garage, I would see if I could go through the back yards. This was a good idea as long as no one looked out their window and saw a shadowy bent over figure traipsing across their lawn or garden. Or, trying to climb over their fence.

I didn't have too much trouble reaching the backyard across from Scooter's garage. This was Amy Hunter's yard. She had a daycare in her home and play structures filled the backyard. Now my problem would be finding a place to settle in for a few hours or as long as it took to see what was happening behind that closed door.

One structure had two slides - one going straight down and the other going in the other direction, making a twist. There was a ladder going up to the top where the children could wait their turn inside a small 'house' that had a pink roof and two tiny windows. I'd found my perfect hiding place. I carefully made my way over to the play area and climbed up the ladder. This was definitely not Charlie's hiding place. It was only large enough for two small children at the most or me.

I snuggled into my hiding spot and watched Scooter's garage from my window. All was quiet except for the muffled sound of voices coming from within. Every so often, someone would laugh and if it were too loud the other person would tell him to shut up. I could hear no female voices. It was warm and actually quite comfortable in my hiding spot except for the faint tinge of urine. I might mention to Amy that her slides could use some bleach.

I must've dozed off because the next thing I knew, the garage door was sliding open with a loud creaking sound and I almost went down the twisted slide. Light from a long florescent bulb streamed out almost reaching my hiding spot. Before I ducked down, I saw that Scooter's car and Calvin's taxi were inside. Calvin was in the process of putting his hubcap back on. I heard him yell at Scooter, "Hey, I'm not finished yet. Shut that door." Scooter replied, "Well, hurry up. We don't have all night."

They didn't speak again. Calvin drove off, driving slower than normal and disappeared down the street. Scooter hit a button on the wall and the garage door went down. That was it. Besides being a disappointing night, my left leg and foot were asleep. It took a few minutes of rubbing my leg and wriggling my toes before I was able to climb down the ladder and walk home. If any of Maxymowich's men were anywhere around, I hadn't seen them.

By the time I'd explained my absence to seven cats and then climbed into bed, it was almost one a.m. A little nip of gin did wonders in helping me go to sleep.

Chapter Twenty Eight

Saturday morning. I usually wake up refreshed, especially if I know there are tourists in town and that I might make enough money in one day to pay for my electrical bill for the month. This Saturday was definitely the exception to the rule. The older I get, the more sleep I seem to need. Six hours, interrupted by two bathroom visits does not make for an energized Mabel Wickles.

Flori phoned at eight thirty to tell me that she was bringing six dozen chocolate chip cookies to the shop.

"Well, it will have to be 'first come, first serve, and no seconds' because I don't want you rushing home to bake more when the first batch is gone," I said.

"I understand, Mabel. However, you know I don't mind making more. It's such an easy recipe. For the real chocolate-chocolate ones, you use chocolate pudding mix. Do you want me to write it up for you?"

"It's all I can do to keep up with the muffin demand but thanks anyway. By the way, Flori, has Jake mentioned anything about Calvin or Scooter lately? You know, like what they've been up to? Or, if they've made any trips together? That sort of thing?"

"I can't remember him saying anything besides all the money Calvin throws around. He did say that Murray was at the café yesterday."

"Really? That's good. He'll get over this much faster if he starts getting out. Sitting watching the water for hours all day is not a way to cope."

"I don't know, Mabel. I think the guys down there wish he went back to sitting and watching the water."

"Why? What happened?"

"Nothing happened because Scully and Jim happened to walk in and stop him."

"Stop him? Stop him from what?"

"From throwing a punch at Calvin."

"Are you serious? Why? What did Calvin say to get him so upset?"

"Jake said that he didn't say a thing, just kind of smirked and that was enough to set Murray off. Murray was sitting with Jake and Denny Wakefield and all of a sudden, he went berserk."

"What did Jim and Scully do?"

"As far as I know, they grabbed Murray and held his arms and then he calmed down. He refused to look at Calvin. He left right away. Jake and the boys tried to make him stay but he never said a word - just walked out."

"I wonder if he's having some sort of breakdown, Flori. I mean, he has gone through a terrible shock - first, Bernie and then, Biscuit. Or, I guess I should say first Biscuit and then, Bernie. Whichever way it was, it was very stressful for him. But, Calvin? Why would he be upset with Calvin? Do you think he believes Calvin is guilty of murdering his friend and his dog?"

"Oh, Mabel, I can't believe Calvin would murder Bernie. I know we don't like him but that doesn't mean he's a murderer."

"I know but that's the only reason I can think of for Murray to do something like that. There's something funny going on with Calvin and Scooter though, Flori. Even Maxymowich is watching them. I think it has to do with their cars. I know that doesn't make sense but it's just a gut feeling that I have. Why would Calvin have his taxi in Scooter's garage and why would he be putting his hubcaps back on? Why would they be off?"

There was a moment of silence.

"Mabel," Flori said. "I have absolutely no idea what you talking about. How did we get from feeling sorry for Murray and his nervous breakdown to Calvin and his hubcaps?"

I suddenly remembered something else. Something that Melanie had told me.

"And, Flori, Bernie was always washing his car. Melanie told me that. It was getting her upset she said." I had no idea where I was going with this but somehow, there had to be some connection. "Why would Bernie suddenly be washing his car all the time?"

"Because it was dirty? You can't condemn people for washing their cars. Besides, what does that have to do with Calvin and Scooter? Probably Calvin had a flat tire and he was changing it in Scooter's garage. Don't you have to take off the hubcaps when you change a tire? I really have no idea what on earth you're talking about."

"I have no idea either but I can't help but feel there's a connection, Flori."

"Well, let me know when you've connected all the dots. I'll see you at nine. Make sure you have coffee on before the crowd bursts through those doors, my friend."

The coffee was on but we were still waiting for the crowd to burst through the doors. By nine-thirty, Flori and I had eaten one dozen cookies. They were the chocolate-chocolate ones and they simply melted in your mouth. To wash them down, we'd polished off two cups of coffee each. I was still waiting for my first customer. Every ten minutes or so, I got up and looked down the street. Mutt must've had the same idea because we met once on the sidewalk.

"Where are all the tourists, Mabel?" he asked. "I stockpiled camping and fishing gear and not one person has come in. It's a beautiful day so what's happened to everyone?"

I looked up and down the street. It reminded me of the hours just before the fight at the OK corral. Deadly silent.

"I don't know, Mutt. It's very strange. It's like a ghost town out there."

"Do you think it has something to do with the murder? Maybe tourists are staying away because of that. What do you think?"

What did I think? Wow, this had been my plan but when did any of my plans ever materialize? Never.

"It could be. Let's face it - would you want to stay in a town where someone had been murdered? I don't mean in a city. If you stayed away from a city because there was a murder, you'd be staying away forever. But, a small town? I doubt I'd want to stay there. How about you, Mutt?"

"I think you're right, Mabel. That's probably the reason. I hope the killer is found soon because you and I could sure use the business, couldn't we?"

Mutt walked into his store with his head hanging down. I took one last look down the street. The only person I could see was Charlie far down the street and even I couldn't yell loud enough to get his attention. Flori was busy packing her cookies back into her Tupperware container when I went back inside.

"What are you doing?" I asked.

She looked up. "There's really no need for me to leave all these cookies here, Mabel. I might as well take some back home for the kids. Some of the grandkids are coming over this afternoon and I never have enough for them to eat. Besides, it doesn't look like anyone is going to be coming in today. I can't figure it out, can you? I've never seen the town so empty on a Saturday in the summer. If this keeps up, Parson's Cove will be a ghost town soon."

"I wish you'd stay a little longer. Do you have to rush home?"

Flori hugged me. "You know I'd love to spend the whole morning with you but I'd better get back. Jake starts to panic if the kids come and I'm not there."

"Jake panics? How the heck did he manage with all his own children? How many did you have anyway, Flori? Six or seven?"

"Mabel, you are hilarious!"

I reached behind and grabbed a handful of Kleenex because when Flori starts laughing hilariously, her tear ducts tend to burst. When she finally calmed down and the wet balled-up tissues were disposed of, I said, "Seriously, Flori, it's seems really weird to me that Jake can't handle his grandkids without you there for support."

"Actually, Jake couldn't handle his own kids without me there, Mabel."

"Really?"

"Really. I must be on my way now. I'll call later. If you're not doing anything tonight, maybe I'll pop over for a visit and a glass of wine. I'll need one after this afternoon is over."

"Sounds good. If you happen to see any humans walking on the street along your way, send them over here. Tell them that there are...," I checked the bowl, "eight cookies left."

Flori left, giggling.

I was on my fifth cookie when the door opened and Esther Flynn walked in.

As I've mentioned, Esther is my nemesis. She has been for over fifty-five years. I'm so used to hating her that I don't think about it anymore. It just comes naturally and seems so much easier than trying to like her or understand her or search for any of her redeeming qualities.

It all started when we were kids. You'd think she would outgrow it but she never did. Everyone said she was jealous because Flori and I were such good friends. It meant that for years I suffered through insults, frogs in my desk, my braids in her inkwell, my locker filled with mice, and as we got older, her schemes got more demonic until the last one she pulled and the one that haunts me to this day. I still can't believe how much time she must've spent copying my handwriting but she did and she had it down to a 't.' So good in fact, that she made two copies of a homework assignment and then secretly removed my copy and put hers in with my name on it. The next day, the principal called me to the office. Why did they think I was the one who copied and not Esther? Because Esther sat in front of me, how could she do the copying? I was given a warning. She got a bit cocky after that and by the time she'd succeeded in crushing me four more times, I was expelled.

"It didn't help that you kicked her in the shins, Mabel." Flori always reminds me. "And, you hit her over the head with your binder and broke her glasses. In fact, if you're being entirely honest, that's the real reason you were expelled."

It's true; I did all that. Nothing to be proud of but I do remember how good it felt at the time.

"So, Miss Wickles, where are all your customers today?" Pushing her glasses up her nose, she continued, "Isn't this your busiest day?" She stood at the door and made a dramatic sweep with her eyes around the room.

"Hmmm. Not a nary customer in sight. My, oh my, what will you do?"

"I'll tell you what we'll do - we'll get rid of every customer who comes in and doesn't buy anything. That's what we'll do." I put my hands on my hips and stared at her. This isn't easy. Not many can outstare Esther Flynn.

"Tut, tut, Mabel. You are assuming that I'm here to gloat but I'll have you know that I'm more mature than you think. That is something I'm sure you would do. I happen to be above that. I also happen to know what happened to all the tourists."

"Really? Now, how would you know that?"

With a look of grand superiority, she lifted her already high nose a little higher and said, "Someone told a lovely elderly couple that there were ruffians cruising our streets at night so they told everyone staying at the Main Street Hotel and all of them left for home."

"I'm so happy you shared that with me, Esther. Please, feel free to walk about my store and if you find something you'd like to purchase, I'll give you ten percent off."

"Fifty."

"Ten."

"Forty."

"Ten."

"Twenty."

"Ten."

"Oh forget it. Everything in this place is so over priced that getting ten percent off is a slap in the face."

"Consider yourself slapped, Esther." I smiled. "Which reminds me of something that I wanted to ask you: What made you go over to Melanie's car and wake her up? You know, when she was sitting in the carwash the day that Bernie was murdered. I'm sure you've told the police already but maybe you left something out. Do you remember exactly how Melanie reacted? In your opinion, was she truly surprised to see Bernie lying, dead in the water, or do you think that she was pretending to be asleep and that she really did hit Bernie over the head with the brick?"

I knew she would never share any information with me but I also knew this was a sure way of getting her out of the store.

She glared, grunted, shook her head and walked out the door, giving it a good slam in the process. I went to the window to watch her. After all, I do enjoy a bit of entertainment in my life. The thermometer that I have attached to my window read eighty-seven degrees. Esther was wearing a two-piece navy knit suit, which almost reached her ankles, a red and white scarf wrapped around her neck with red flat-heeled patent leather shoes and a wide brimmed white hat. She carried a white patent purse. Just watching her made me walk over and turn the air conditioner up.

Ten minutes after Esther made her escape, Sheriff Smee walked in. He was still wearing his summer police attire – no tie, no gun and sandals. His top two shirt buttons were undone and he'd rolled his shirtsleeves up to the elbow. He still looked hot and uncomfortable.

He took off his cap and fanned his face.

"Man, I can't take much more of this heat, Mabel. You got a cold beer?"

"You know I don't have a cold beer."

"What do you have? Got some soda pop?"

"I'll tell you what I've got – hot coffee and three chocolate cookies."

He sighed and put one of the chairs in front of the a/c.

"Bring it on. Guess that'll have to do."

A few minutes later, he'd gobbled down the last of the cookies and drained his coffee.

"Well," I said. "Doesn't look like you were too hard done by. Those cookies disappeared fast."

"They were small. Besides, when I'm frustrated I eat." He held his cup out for a refill. "I can't figure out why they haven't found Bernie's killer yet. How can it be so hard? It has to be someone who probably walks past us on the street every day."

"Murray said he thought it was a stranger."

Reg shook his head. "I wish it were but I don't think so, Mabel." He stared down at the floor. "Nope, it has to be someone here in Parson's Cove."

"Did Prunella ever say who hit her with the frying pan?"

"No, she still claims that she fell and crawled to the bed. Maybe she really believes that she did; she was pretty high on drugs and liquor."

"If there weren't any prints on the glass tumbler on the table and none on the frying pan, there's no one to even question. I wonder if there were any witnesses though. Someone who might've seen a person going into her place. I should ask Charlie."

Reg stood up. "I'll take a walk around town and question a few people. I think Maxymowich had his men talking to almost everyone but you never know; they might open up more to me." He put his cap on and walked over to the door. "I'll see what I can do."

"Don't sound so discouraged. There has to be clues staring us in the face. We just can't see them yet."

I looked out the window.

"Reg, look! There's Calvin's taxi parked across the street. Wonder what he's up to? I'd sure like to know what he does at night in Scooter's garage. Those two are up to something. I wish you'd go and check them out."

"I'll tell you, Mabel, if the Captain suspects them of something, I'm staying out of it. Besides, it's not that easy to get a search warrant anymore. If I went to the garage, they wouldn't have to let me in and there's nothing I could do about it."

"I don't know; that doesn't sound fair somehow."

"I know. Say, is that one of your cats over there by Calvin's taxi?"

"I'd like to say probably not because my cats stay in the yard but it does look like Sammy. I don't know. All white cats look alike."

"Yeah, but who else has a white cat? What's he doing anyway? Looks like he's trying to scratch off Calvin's hubcap."

"I'd better go over and get him before Calvin comes back. This time, he'll give Sammy a kick for sure."

"This time?"

"I didn't tell you? Sammy snuck on the bus when we went to the city and for some reason he wanted to sniff Calvin's shoes. Well, I guess I don't blame Calvin; after all, it's hard to drive with a cat attacking your feet. When Calvin went to kick him, all the old people got into an uproar. That's one reason why he lost his job."

Reg looked out. "I think you're too late, Mabel. Calvin's coming back to his car."

Calvin didn't see the cat until he walked around to the driver's side. I watched in dread as he grabbed my cat by the scruff of the neck. Fortunately, Sheriff Smee is faster on his feet than I am. He was out the door and racing across the street before I could even get my mouth closed.

Since Reg was handling it, I thought it might be wise to keep out of sight. (Flori would've been proud). It gave me great satisfaction to watch him grab Sammy out of Calvin's clutches. I had no idea what the two men were saying to each other but it was quite animated. Twice Sammy jumped out of Reg's arms and went back to the hubcaps. I was really beginning to think I had a demented cat. Well, if Flori could put up with her children whom I thought were demented at times, I guess I could put up with one mentally challenged cat.

In a few minutes, Reg was back with Sammy in a football hold. Obviously, the cat didn't like taking the place of a football. His ears were back and there was a low growl coming from somewhere in his throat.

"Here," Reg said. "Take this cat before he attacks me. If this were a pit bull, you'd be in real trouble, Mabel. This is a killer cat, do you know that?"

I grabbed Sammy, who stopped growling immediately and looked at me, as if to say, 'it's about time you came to my rescue.' I'd love to say that he started to purr and rub his chin against mine but he didn't. He jumped down and ran into the backroom where I keep a bowl of water and some dry cat food in case any of my cats come for a visit.

"He's not a killer cat. There's something about Calvin that he doesn't like. Or, something. Something in his car and on his shoes." I stared at Reg. "There's something in Calvin's boots and Calvin's hubcaps that is attracting my cat to them, Reg."

"Like what, catnip?"

"I'm thinking more like drugs."

Reg's mouth dropped open. "I wonder if you're right, Mabel. Whatever it is, your cat can't leave it alone, that's for sure."

"I bet that's why Captain Maxymowich is watching them. They might be tied up with the murder. I wouldn't be surprised. Maybe Bernie was selling drugs too. Melanie said that he was always washing his car. Maybe he was washing away the evidence. I think we're getting some place now." I looked up at the

Sheriff. "What do you think, Reg? Isn't this starting to make sense to you?"

"You could be right, but so far this is just our imagination. We'll have to find proof. This means, you don't talk to anyone about what we suspect, you got that? Not even Flori. If you do and word gets around, the whole case will go down the tube. You understand?"

"Of course, I understand. But, it is exciting when you start to put the pieces together, isn't it?"

"Mabel, for all we know, Sammy might smell something entirely different. Maybe some other cat left its mark. In fact, you should keep an eye on him to see what he's sniffing out."

We both looked over at Sammy, now curled up on Reg's chair. He looked up and glared at us.

"Sammy," I said. "If you solve this murder case, I'll give you gourmet cat food for a whole year."

Sammy's tail switched back and forth as if he didn't believe a word that I said.

Chapter Twenty Nine

Flori arrived at my house a little after seven. I was in the kitchen. She didn't even stop; she kept walking into the living room, ordering as she went, "Mabel, bring me a large glass of wine. I never want to see my grandchildren again as long as I live."

She said the 'as long as I live' from the living room couch. I could hear her shoes hitting the floor and the couch groaning as she sprawled back into it. Two of my cats walked over and looked at me, enquiringly. "It's okay," I told them. "I'm very happy to have you instead of grandchildren." This should have made them happy but instead, they walked to the fridge and demanded food. "On second thought," I said, "maybe I should have goldfish."

I handed Flori her wine in the largest glass I could find.

"So, what's the problem? I thought you adored all those grandkids."

Flori reached down and pulled two tissues from her bra. She patted her forehead. "I did. I don't know what's happened to them. Oh Mabel, those sweet innocent children are turning into juvenile zombies."

"Watch the wine, Flori." Her glass kept moving up and down with each dramatic gesture.

"They are rude, inconsiderate and lazy. That's all I can say. No 'please' and 'thank you'; all of them want to be the first to get anything and all they do is sit around in the house and play with their phones and some other thing they call an iPad." Desperation showed in her eyes. "What's going to happen to them?"

I took a drink of wine. My supply of Sadie MacIntosh's homemade chokecherry wine was coming to an end. Only six bottles to last until fall. Every year, I let Sadie put some of her preservatives in my store in exchange for her wine. Usually I end up buying most of it so she won't feel too bad so technically, I pay for the wine. Fortunately, she knows how to make wine so I don't mind.

"Probably nothing will happen to them, Flori. Your kids went through that stage too. At least, these kids are in sight. Yours weren't always. Remember when little Jake stole a skateboard? And, let's not forget the girls – remember when Rachel got that tattoo and you didn't find out until just a year or so ago." I took another swallow and looked over at Flori.

By the look of dismay on her face, you'd think she was on the Titanic and the captain told her they'd just hit an iceberg.

"Tattoo? What tattoo?"

"You knew about Rachel's tattoo, Flori. I'm sure I told you. Or, was it Jake? Oh, sorry, maybe I told Jake. Anyway it's over and done with and it shows how kids can do foolish things but change."

Tears were welling up in Flori's eyes. "How could you have kept this from me, Mabel?" The tears flowed, the wine spilled and I drank.

When the room was quiet again, I said, "I guess that's why I didn't want to tell you."

I filled her glass again and handed her a tea towel to sop up any puddles of wine that were lying around.

"That isn't all that I'm upset about, Mabel. That's bad enough but I got a phone call from Mr. Kinney at the retirement home and he said that he won't need me to go with the seniors. Not only that, he said Calvin will be taking them again. I can't believe it." She burst into tears again.

"Calvin is going with them?"

She nodded in between hiccoughs.

"I thought they didn't want him anymore. Did the lawsuit scare them?"

She shrugged and nodded in between sniffles and snorts. "I guess."

"Oh boy, those old people won't be too happy with that. But, why can't you go? Are they sending them with Calvin and nobody else?"

This time, she shook her head, took one last sniffle and said, "No, he said they have another lady all picked out." She wailed. I waited. "Why don't they want me anymore, Mabel? I thought I was very good with all of them."

"You were. You were better than anyone else was. I don't know, Flori. This is very strange. But, don't worry, I'll ask Reg about it."

"Oh no, don't ask him. Please, don't tell anyone how I feel. Jake doesn't even know. I mean it, Mabel, don't tell anyone, okay?"

I smiled. "Okay. I won't. Let's finish our wine and talk about positive things. For instance, Bernie's murder. Reg and I really do think we're getting closer to finding the killer. Do you want to hear about it?"

"Mabel, when I say that I want to talk about positive things, I don't mean murder. Isn't there anything good to talk about?"

"Well, Esther was in today and told me why all the tourists left. I guess that's positive."

"Why did all the tourists leave?"

"Some old couple said that, as Esther put it, ruffians were roaming the streets of Parson's Cove so they decided to return after the murderer has been captured."

"There aren't ruffians roaming the streets at night. Where would they come up with a story like that?"

"Oh, who knows? The world is full of silly people."

Chapter Thirty

Sunday morning.

Sunday morning arrived with its usual warm welcome. I tried to sleep longer but by seven-thirty, it was already stuffy and hot in my bedroom. The only cat who braved the heat and stayed with me for the night was Phyl but before six, she got up, stretched the full length of her body, jumped off the bed and left me. The small fan on the table faced my head and blew hot air in my ear. Finally, I gave in, got out of bed and had a lukewarm shower before heading downstairs.

While the coffee brewed, I fed the cats. By the time the coffee was ready, the cats were ready to escape. I opened the door and they scattered like seven leaves in the wind. I guess after spending so much time together in the house, they need some 'alone time.' I know I sure did.

It was so much cooler in the shade outside than inside that I decided to enjoy my coffee sitting in my lawn chair in the back yard. I don't have an especially great lawn or flowerbed but I do try to keep everything looking as manicured as I can. It's nothing like my father used to have. For example, I don't bother with a vegetable garden any more. I replaced it with a perennial garden. Usually, it's blooming with flowers of every color but this summer because of the long dry hot period, I'm afraid most of the plants were looking dull and droopy. Some people get up and water early in the morning but I don't. Every plant and tree in my yard has to be hardy and survive on its own. Mostly because

I can't afford a huge water bill to make my backyard that very few people see, look great. Unfortunately, I've found that the hardiest plants in my backyard are the quack grass and dandelions.

There's a fence separating my yard and Krueger's yard. My father and Mr. Krueger built it over forty years ago. They don't make fences like that anymore. I've added a few coats of paint over the years but it's still sturdy and, as they say, it has endured the tests of time. There are several shrubs along the fence. I try to plant ones that blossom, smell nice, and last forever. For that reason, I have five lilac bushes planted exactly twelve feet apart along the inside of the fence. For several weeks in June the fragrance from the lilacs is so strong that I almost have to wear a clothespin on my nose every time I go outside. Not that I don't like the scent – I love it; however, it turns out that it makes me sneeze but I don't have the heart to rip out all of those shrubs. Besides, it does give me some privacy. From May to September, someone is usually renting Krueger's house. Sometimes, I end up with noisy rambunctious neighbors who have three or four kids. Usually, however, it's a couple of old coots who fish all day. They spend the days fishing and the evenings sitting in the backyard, drinking. There's an old homemade barbeque pit back there and if things get too loud, I give Reg a call. He doesn't appreciate it but I've found that all he has to do is come into my backyard and peer over the fence. Within ten minutes, everyone evacuates and only silence fills the night.

Now, as I sat drinking my first cup of coffee, I was thinking how lovely and quiet it was with the latest renters. I wasn't even sure if Jeff's wife had arrived. They were definitely my kind of people. Just as I was thinking this and at the same time watching Sammy trying to sneak through the fence, I heard their back door open. A lilac bush hindered most of my view but I caught a glimpse of a young woman with white blond hair walking on the sidewalk along the back of the house. Perhaps, if I saw her outside again, I'd yell over and introduce myself.

I waited until after ten to make a visit to Melanie. Reg hadn't called so I didn't know if he went over to see her or not. Besides, sometimes a woman will open up more to another woman. I wasn't sure how it would go so I decided that I'd better take some muffins with me. I always feel that if they don't let me in, it still opens the way for the next visit.

It turned out that I wouldn't have needed them because before I even knocked, Melanie opened the door.

"Mabel," she said. "I've been waiting and waiting for you to visit." She grabbed my arm and pulled me inside.

The kitchen was cool and dark. The whole house felt cold and gloomy. Even if all the blinds were up and the sun was shining in, I think it wouldn't have made a difference. She kept her hand on my arm and steered me into the living room. We sat down on the couch.

"Are you all alone?" I asked.

She nodded. There were tears in her eyes. She blinked them away.

"You know I have to stay here, don't you? I can't leave Parson's Cove. Did you know that, Mabel?"

"Well, I sort of figured that out. Don't they have any other suspects in Bernie's murder?"

She sniffed and shook her head. "If they do, no one tells me." The tears she'd been blinking away now poured out. I put my bag of muffins on the coffee table and handed her a Kleenex from a box on the table. I guess she was keeping them handy.

"Oh Mabel, why did I ever make that stupid confession? What was I thinking? It was all so confusing. I threw that stone at him. For some reason, I thought I must've killed him. I mean, who else would?"

I shook my head. "I don't know. Something must've been going on. Something you weren't aware of. You said that Bernie was always washing his car. When did that start, do you remember?"

She was silent for a few minutes, thinking.

"I don't know what that has to do with the murder but Mabel, I do remember when Bernie started acting weird."

"He started acting weird?"

She nodded. "It kind of struck me strange at the time too, now that I think about it. He took an old pair of shoes over to Scooter to have him replace the soles. When he picked them up a couple of days later, he came home with the wrong pair. They looked exactly like Bernie's but they were someone else's. Bernie was very upset because the soles were falling off this pair so he thought Scooter was pulling a fast one on him. The next thing you know, Scooter is phoning, cussing and swearing and he got Bernie all upset. I mean, what's the big deal about an old pair of stinky boots, right? You'd think Bernie was the one who'd made the mistake. Anyway, Bernie hurried back with those boots and I didn't see him until the next morning."

"Are you serious? Weren't you worried?"

Melanie looked down at her hands. "I guess I might as well tell you, Mabel, that Bernie and I were having some marriage problems." She raised her head. "There were quite a few nights where he would go out and not come home so, no I wasn't worried. Angry? Yes. I always wondered if he was out drinking with his buddies or if he was with some woman." She stopped to wipe away a few tears that trickled down her cheek. "I was thinking about divorcing him and I guess eventually it would've come to that. At first, he wanted to go for marriage counseling but the last month or so, he showed no interest in saving our marriage at all. He said I could do whatever I wanted." Tears ran down her face but she didn't seem to notice. "That's not what a woman wants to hear. I wanted to stick it out. I thought if we could get through this bad time, things could only get better."

"What did your parents think?"

"My parents? They've hated Bernie from the start. To begin with, they're very prejudiced. Did you know that? Remember Beulah Henry? They wouldn't even buy any of her produce when she displayed it outside your store in the summer because she was black."

"You're kidding! They hated Beulah? She was murdered and her own son was involved, how could anyone hate her?"

"I know, Mabel, but I've lived with it all my life."

"How do they feel about someone killing Bernie?"

"Well, they try to be sympathetic but I know that deep inside, they're probably glad that he's gone and they don't have to deal with him anymore."

"What do you mean, deal with him?"

She sighed. "Bernie brought on a lot of his own problems. He didn't practice his faith but he liked to pretend in front of my parents. When he came for a meal, he wouldn't eat any pork and my mother would make sure she always had pork or ham just to bug him."

"Do you think your brother might've hit Bernie on the head in a fit of rage or frustration?"

"I don't know. If he did, I'm sure it would be by accident but he would never let me take the blame. No, it couldn't have been Steve."

"You said that Bernie started acting weird after Scooter gave him the wrong boots. Why do you think that was?"

She shook her head. "I don't know. He started spending more and more time with them. I'd hear him arguing over the phone but when I walked in, he'd hang up."

"How do you know he was talking to Scooter?"

"I'd hear his name. It was either Scooter or Calvin."

"Really? Scooter or Calvin? I wonder what they would be arguing about?"

"Money. At least, that's what I think. Bernie was always concerned about money. He bragged to me about showing up my parents. He always thought they had lots of money but were just stingy. My parents aren't rich, Mabel, but for some reason Bernie thought so. I think maybe that's why he married me."

"Well, that and agreeing to swim in the nude probably helped."

"Don't remind me. How could I be so foolish, Mabel?"

"You were young, that's all."

"But look at you, Mabel. You're the smart one. I wish I were you."

"You want to live alone with seven cats?"

I didn't want to add to her depression but at the moment that sounded pretty good to me too.

"I'm allergic to cats but you know what I mean. You were strong enough to fend off all the men who were after you and you stayed single. I think that's wonderful. Now, look at you. You have your own business and you've solved murder cases. You should be so proud of yourself."

Melanie was revealing things to me that I'd never known. For instance, when were all those men chasing after me? It's true, I think I did make the most of my singleness but that doesn't mean that I didn't feel sorry for myself once in awhile along the way.

"Melanie," I said. "You keep looking at your watch. Are you expecting someone?"

She quickly covered her watch with her sleeve again. "I'm sorry; I didn't want to be so obvious but Captain Maxymowich and Reg are supposed to come over this morning."

"Reg? Reg is coming with Maxymowich?"

She nodded. "Apparently, Reg asked to come over too. He thought I'd feel more at ease with a policeman from Parson's Cove and I told the Captain that I would. Do you think it would be a good idea for them to see you here?"

I smiled and stood up. "Probably not. By the way, I think you should tell them about Bernie's involvement with Calvin and Scooter. And, the shoes. Don't forget to tell them about Bernie getting the wrong shoes. I have a feeling that's going to be important."

"Do you really think so? I wonder if I should tell him about the hubcaps?"

I sat down again. "Hubcaps? What about them?"

"Well, besides washing the car when it didn't need it, he started removing the hub caps from his car, cleaning them, and putting them back on all the time. I asked him why he was doing it but he told me to mind my own business."

"Did you ever think they might be hiding drugs in the hubcaps?"

She looked at me in astonishment. "Drugs? You mean, like cocaine or marijuana? Of course not. Why would they bring drugs to Parson's Cove? Mabel, who in our little town would buy drugs?"

"I don't think Parson's Cove is the perfect little place you think it is. We don't live in a bubble here, Melanie. Besides, we have many tourists all summer. What if some of them like having their drugs brought right to them? I think there might be a lucrative drug market here."

We heard a car door slam and watched Maxymowich walking up to the front door with Sheriff Smee several feet behind. I have to admit that I was proud of my sheriff. He found a very legitimate way of getting in to see Melanie. I hoped that he'd learn even more than I had.

I escaped the living room just as the doorbell rang and went out the back door. As I snuck down the lane, I detoured down Scooter's lane. His wife, Betty, happened to be putting out her garbage when I walked past.

I think when we see someone putting out the garbage, we have the natural instinct to look and see what it is. Betty and Scooter had exactly what I envisioned. She worked nights so had no time to cook and he was lazy so all they ate were packaged and junk food. It was disappointing to know that someone who worked in the hospital wouldn't eat better though. Not that I wanted to stare but I hadn't seen that many empty doughnut and cookie cartons in a long time. This is not counting what Flori and I eat because everything we consume is made from real butter, sugar and eggs.

"Betty," I said, in a loud voice but not too loud that I would make her jump. "How are you? Haven't seen you around for awhile; although I guess that's because you're busy working nights."

Betty looked up. She looked like a night worker - dark around the eyes with tired gray skin.

"Oh, hi Mabel." She slowly straightened up and even though she didn't say her back was aching, I could feel that it was. "Yeah, I don't see much of anyone. If I didn't need the extra cash that comes from working nights, believe me, I would never do it. Scooter insists that I quit after next year. I don't know what he's thinking. I doubt the shoe repair business is going to pick up." She laughed. Not an infectious laugh - you knew she didn't expect you to laugh in return.

"I don't know how you've done it all these years. Even at your age, I don't think I could've handled it." I gave her one of my 'encouraging you to talk' smiles. "How is Scooter's business doing anyway? Seems he's always busy in that garage of yours."

She shrugged. "Things have picked up lately. At least, he claims we'll have enough saved to go on a vacation this summer. I could sure use one."

She reached down to pick up a flattened cookie bag that had dropped to the ground and stuffed it inside the recycling box that sat beside the old dented garbage can.

"Scooter must really like his sweets," I said. "I should get Flori to bake some cinnamon buns for him. They are so much better than those store-bought goodies."

She smiled. "I know we eat too much junk. I haven't baked in years. I don't think I'd even know how anymore."

"Well, if Scooter is right about his business picking up, maybe you can retire and do all the baking you'd like."

"Wouldn't that be a dream? I hope it comes true because I'm sure sick of working so much. I shouldn't say that though, Mabel, because I do love my job. It's just the night work that wears me out."

"I'm wondering what kind of people get their shoes repaired nowadays. Of course, I'm always in sneakers so I wear them until they fall apart. I mean, who wears shoes that cost enough to have repaired? Why not buy a new pair?"

"I know what you mean. I don't even get Scooter to fix my shoes. He gets quite a few orders for work boots from the city. He said he had some kind of contract with a company. To tell you the truth, Mabel, I was so tired I didn't really pay much attention to what he was telling me."

"A contract from the city? I would say that's the way to go. Good for him. How, on earth, would he get the boots delivered? You know, all that travelling - would a person make anything after you paid for the gas?"

"I have no idea but I'm sure he's hatched up some plan."

"I'm sure he has. Maybe Calvin helps him out. They're together quite a bit."

She made a face. "I think he has too much to do with that guy but he's a grown man; he should be old enough to choose his own friends, I guess." She closed the lid on the garbage can. "I'd better get back to my cleaning. Nice talking with you, Mabel."

"Nice chatting with you too, Betty." I started to walk away but turned back and said, "How come you have to clean when Scooter's at home all the time?"

This time she did a genuine laugh. "Yeah, right. Thanks for sharing the joke of the day with me."

Chapter Thirty One

I felt that we were progressing well in the case. The murderer hadn't been caught but there were obviously nefarious happenings going on in Parson's Cove. Scooter and Calvin were involved in something and Bernie was in on it too. Or, I should say, 'had been' in on it. Did Bernie double cross them and one of them ended up killing him? Why would someone kill him behind the carwash though? Especially if Melanie was sitting in the car. Wasn't that a bit daring? She could've popped around the corner or opened the back door at any time. Maybe Bernie was doing a drug deal and something went wrong. Maybe. Maybe. Maybe.

It was after supper before Reg phoned.

"So?" I said. "What did you find out from Maxymowich?"

"Not much, Mabel. They're pretty tight-lipped about it all. Melanie did tell us about the shoes and hubcaps but Maxymowich told me afterwards that they'd checked out Scooter's garage and house but there was no evidence of drugs of any kind."

"Really? Scooter must've known they were watching and cleaned everything up. It has to be drugs, Reg. What else could it be?"

"I don't know but I do know one thing, Mabel, we can't prove anything because your cat is intrigued with some odor. Besides, I'm sure that drugs would be in a plastic bag or a container of some sort so how could your cat smell anything through that?"

"I don't know. I'm very disappointed. I thought there would be drugs in those shoes and hubcaps. Whatever we do, we have to find out what those two were hiding because I'm sure that's why Bernie was killed."

"I'll give you a warning - don't mention your cat to the Captain."

"Why?"

"Because I hinted at it and he almost choked, he was laughing so hard."

"Is that so? Well, what if Murray's dog was sniffing out something and that's why it got killed?"

There was a moment of silence on the other end. There was also a moment of silence on my end. The words had just popped out but they made perfect sense. Why would anyone hit an old friendly dog on the head that had never hurt anyone in its life – unless that dog was sniffing out something that it shouldn't be?

I knew then what I would have to do. Somehow, I'd have to get to either Scooter's garage or Calvin's boots and take my cat with me.

"Reg," I said. "I have a plan."

For once, the Sheriff thought that I had a good idea.

Chapter Thirty Two

Sammy and I were to meet Reg at midnight. He would pick me up at my house and we'd proceed with caution (in other words, with the headlights off), first to Calvin's house and then if his taxi wasn't parked outside, to Scooter's garage.

Sammy knew something was up. Perhaps, it was because all the other cats were allowed outside and he was forced to stay in. I definitely didn't trust him to return home on time. To make everything look normal, I shut all my lights off by ten and wandered around the house in the dark.

There were lights on in the house behind mine. I still hadn't met Jeff's wife so I thought that to pass the time, I would keep my eye on the house. Maybe I'd catch a glimpse of her through the window so I pulled down my mini blinds and peeked through the slats. Really, what else was there for me to do?

Good thing that I did too. It was about ten thirty when I happened to look out the window. Who do you think I saw? Good old Scooter and Calvin entering Krueger's backdoor. I also happen to know when someone is sneaking around. Why else would they both stand on the step and watch my house until the door opened for them?

I should've given Reg a call right then but I didn't want to leave my post. They weren't in the house for very long. Just in and out. I'd say long enough to make a drug deal though.

"You sure it was Scooter and Calvin?" were the first words out of Sheriff Smee's mouth when I told him what I'd seen.

"Of course, it was. It's pretty easy to pick those two out even if it's in the dark. Besides, the kitchen window gave enough light for me to see their profiles."

"I know it looks suspicious but I'm sure the cops did a thorough search. You know Maxymowich. I can't see him missing anything."

"What exactly did they find?"

We were now coasting along on Scooter's back lane. Reg was driving his SUV. He'd left the cruiser parked in front of his house so people would think he was home. Besides, there's no way you can sneak around town in a police cruiser. I offered to use my car but Reg said my 1969 Buick would be more obvious than the cruiser. However, I have a feeling that if I'd told him he could drive, he probably would've said okay.

"I don't think they found anything that meant anything."

"Well, just tell me what he told you. There were no drugs of any kind?"

"The only drugs that they found were in the house and in the glove compartment of the car."

"What kind of drugs?"

"Nothing illegal, Mabel. Drugs for diabetes, that's all."

"Who's diabetic?"

"I think Betty must be."

"That's strange because when I was talking to her today, she didn't mention anything like that."

"You were talking to her today?"

"Yeah. She was putting her garbage and recycling out. I'll tell you, it was mostly folded doughnut and cake cartons. She said she didn't bake anymore so they ate store bought baking. I offered Flori's cinnamon buns but if she or Scooter were diabetic, I'm sure she would've said something. Besides, she's a nurse and she'd be a very foolish one to have that much junk food in her home if either one was diabetic."

"I know that doesn't make sense, Mabel, but some people aren't too smart when it comes to health. Sometimes the worst ones are those who look after other people's health. She could be diabetic and still buy cakes for Scooter. Maybe he insists. Or, maybe he buys it."

"I guess you're right." I still couldn't help but feel that if Betty was diabetic, she would've mentioned it. Women share things like that. In case someone found out that she was, she'd want to make sure everyone knew the sweet treats were not for her.

We slid slowly to a stop a few houses down from Scooter's garage. Calvin had parked his taxi close to the door so vehicles could drive past. There was a light on in the garage so the two men would be inside.

"Come on," Reg said. "Bring your cat."

Sammy, who had been thoroughly enjoying this outing, leaped out of my grasp as soon as the door was open an inch, squeezed through and jumped to the ground. My heart sank. If ever I felt like killing a cat, it was now. Not that I ever would, it was a fleeting fancy.

"Mabel," Reg yelled. "Catch that damn cat! Why'd you let him go?"

If ever I felt like killing a cop. Fear not - only a fleeting fancy.

"I'll have you know, Reg Smee, I did not let him go on purpose. Lower your voice. Do you want the whole neighborhood to see us?"

We both looked down the lane. Thankfully Sammy is the one who has the good sniffer because he's my only white cat and he was easy to spot in the moonlight. He was heading straight for Calvin's taxi.

Reg grabbed a large screwdriver from off the dashboard and we raced after Sammy.

As before, the cat couldn't get enough of Calvin's hubcaps. He was going frantic, scratching and sniffing.

"Reg," I whispered. "Do you hear Sammy? He's purring."

Reg bent down and began removing the hubcap. Sammy was going crazy. The cap fell to the ground with a clatter. We held our breath. Sammy was concerned. He was ripping away at the paper bag that held something very smelly.

"Phew," I said. "Now I know why Sammy loved the smell of this; it smells like fish."

"Old dead fish." Reg stopped breathing through his nose and started breathing through his mouth. "You hang on to your cat, Mabel, and I'll take one of these small packets. I'll put the rest back."

Sammy wasn't too pleased being held again. "Reg," I whispered, "Give him a piece of brown paper. I won't have so much trouble carrying him to the car then."

He ripped off a small piece of paper and handed it to me. "It's just the paper that smells anyway."

Sammy was quite content to chew on the piece of brown paper all the way to the car. I would be content if the smell of dead fish didn't stay in my nostrils. What were those men doing? Were they putting drugs into dead fish smelling bags so the drugs couldn't be detected? Surely, they could've used some of Betty's perfume instead.

I sat down and started to buckle up when I saw Reg racing towards me. At the same time, I saw the garage door start to rise. It had been a long time since I'd seen my sheriff run that fast. He jumped in and started the truck up before the door closed. I'm sure his foot was dangling outside as we made our getaway. The last I saw as Reg turned the truck around was Calvin standing outside the garage yelling something.

"What happened?" I asked as we sped towards my place.

"They heard me putting the hubcap back on," he said. "I had to give it a kick with my foot and they must've heard that. Darn thing wouldn't go on."

"Well, I don't think he could see who we were. I wonder if they'll figure out what we were up to?"

He shrugged. "I don't think it will take long. That's the first place they'll look now."

It took only about three minutes to get to my house. I looked at the clock on the dash. It wasn't quite one yet.

I jumped out. Sammy went off into the night with the brown paper in his mouth. Undoubtedly, he'd be bragging to every alley cat that he could find.

"Let me know what kind of drugs those are as soon as you can, Reg. Maybe this is where Prunella bought her drugs. This could be a real big drug bust for you and me."

"I'll take them over to the lab at the hospital first thing in the morning," he said.

Before he ripped out of the driveway, I saw Hilda Whinegate's lights go on and I knew by ten tomorrow morning half of Parson's Cove would think I'd been out carousing with some male stranger.

Chapter Thirty Three

Monday morning

"What, in heaven's name, were you thinking?" Flori was yelling in my ear. The phone was about six inches away and it still hurt. Not the words, the sound.

It wasn't seven yet and I hadn't finished my first cup of coffee. The sky was dark and it looked like one of those dreary, damp, depressing, dismal days. I was glad I didn't have to drag myself to work. Monday was always an unprofitable day for me. Flori was concerned at first when I closed for the day but when she realized I was spending more money turning the lights on than what I was taking in, she couldn't understand why I hadn't done it years before. Of course, now that everyone else decided to follow suit, Parson's Cove is a quiet place on a Monday.

"What are you talking about, Flori?" I asked.

"Mabel, you didn't come home until the wee hours in the morning. Hilda called me not five minutes ago to see if I knew anything about it. I can't believe that you're leading a double life."

I waited because I knew what was coming. The clock said ten to seven. The tears would last five, the coughing and hiccoughing another five and then the sniffling.

(Through the years, many have asked me about Flori's crying habits. Some have even suggested psychotherapy. Since this has been her personality for as long as I remember, however, it really doesn't bother me. She contributes all my idiosyncrasies to being an

only child and I contribute all hers to being an only
child for four years and then having six siblings to deal
with.)

At three minutes past seven, Flori resumed speaking.

"I'm sorry, Mabel, but you've been my very best
friend for so many years and you know that I've shared
everything with you."

"I know, Flori. You've shared things with me that
you didn't even share with Jake. And, you've shared
things about Jake that make me blush just to think
about."

"Then, why? Why?"

"Why what, Flori?"

There was a stunned silence.

"Why what? Why were you coming home at three in
the morning? Not only that, you were in an old army
Jeep with no muffler and were waking up the whole
neighborhood. And, who was the handsome stranger
who dropped you off at your door?"

This was too much. Hilda had outdone herself this
time. I'd have to congratulate her when I saw her. I was
laughing so hard I had to put my coffee cup down.

"Mabel, are you there? What's the matter? Are you
okay?"

"I'm fine."

"You sound like you're crying."

"No. I'm laughing like you. In fact, I'm having the
best laugh that I've had in years."

"Okay, tell me the story. Surely, Hilda couldn't get it
all wrong. What time did you really get in and who was
the handsome man who brought you home?"

"I have to admit it was late, Flori. Later than you
would be pleased with."

"I knew it. I knew it. Oh what will the neighbors
think?" The tears started anew. I waited.

When there was a lull, I said, "It was after midnight and the handsome stranger was Sheriff Smee. The old army Jeep was his SUV and as far as I know, it did have a muffler. Our romantic evening was spent doing surveillance."

"What do you mean, you were doing surveillance? What, on earth, are you getting involved in, Mabel? Reg is the sheriff so he can do things like that but you can't. Do you understand? You just can't."

"Okay, well, it wasn't really surveillance. We took Sammy to check out Calvin's taxi."

"Oh my word, now I've heard everything. You have your poor innocent cat involved?"

"Well, one thing, Flori, we now know why Sammy was so attracted to Calvin's hubcaps and boots - Scooter and Calvin hide drugs that smell like dead fish."

"What kind of drugs smell like dead fish?"

"We don't know yet. Reg is having them checked out. We took one stash from the hubcap."

"You stole one stash? What if Calvin finds out?"

"Flori, Reg is a cop. You have a tendency to repeat that but then forget."

"So, how are we going to get rid of the gossip, Mabel?"

"I have no idea but I'm sure you'll think of something. Why don't you go along with it? You know, let everyone think that I have an amazingly handsome boyfriend."

"Oh Mabel, that's disgusting."

"Thanks a lot. You don't think I could have an amazingly handsome boyfriend?"

"No, I don't mean that; I mean calling Reg, amazingly handsome is disgusting."

"Don't tell Beth that, Flori.

"No, she always thought Reg was a catch." She sighed. "I used to secretly dream of Jake being a policeman. Did I ever tell you that, Mabel?"

"Yes, I believe you did. My imagination shut down when you started talking about handcuffs."

"Oh, Mabel, you're so funny. By the way, what are you going to do now? Please, tell me you're not going to do any more surveillance - or whatever you call it. I'm so afraid that you're going to get hurt one of these days."

"You don't have to worry; my next step is to grab a coffee and a book and head back to bed. I shouldn't get into too much trouble doing that."

"Oh you silly thing, you know what I mean. I mean, what kind of trouble are you going to get into? I always thought you and Reg were almost enemies. You never speak too well of him, you know. How come you're all buddy-buddy now?" She hesitated for a second or two. "You aren't using him, are you, Mabel?"

"Of course, I'm not using him, as you so nastily put it. I'll have you know, Reg and I work very well together. Besides, we have only each other. Maxymowich and his crew have taken over the case."

"Mabel, I'm going to say something and I want you to listen very carefully." She stopped and caught her breath. "You don't seem to understand - this is not *your* case. Maxymowich is a police officer and so is Sheriff Smee but you, Mabel – you are simply a storeowner. You have nothing to do with crime." Another brief pause. "Why can't you understand that?"

"Everything you said is true, Flori. I do understand that. It's just that I have the instincts of a police officer. In another life, I'm sure that's what I would be. Not everyone thinks like us."

"Us? Who's 'us?'"

"Well, Maxymowich and me. And, sometimes Reg. Maybe Miss Marple. Definitely, Chief Inspector Jury."

Flori sighed loud enough for the cats to hear. "All right, I know when I'm beat. Go, have your coffee and delve into your Martha Grimes book."

"Flori, I'm so proud. How did you know I was reading Martha Grimes?"

"Don't make fun. We're reading *Jerusalem Inn* for the book club this week."

"Okay, talk later. Don't worry about me. I won't be getting into any trouble."

Chapter Thirty Four

The heat zapped my energy and the cool dull weather made me lethargic. I'm not sure what was needed to get me moving. Finally, by noon I overcame inertia and started my usual Monday cleaning. It consists mostly of cleaning up after the cats. If there were such a thing as cat hair-filled pillows, I could start up my own business. As it is, all they do is plug up my vacuum. So, I dusted, vacuumed, cleaned out the litter boxes, washed out the cats' dishes and cleaned my bathroom. It was one by then and I didn't have the incentive to go on.

I phoned Flori but Jake said she was indisposed.

"What the heck does that mean?" I asked.

In a subdued voice, he said, "She's in the bathroom, crying."

"I thought she only cried when I talked to her."

"Are you serious? She cries when anyone talks to her. This time, Mabel, she has good reason."

"Really? What's the reason? Does it have anything to do with me and Reg?"

"Oh that. No, it doesn't have anything to do with you two; although I don't know what you were thinking. If Scooter and Calvin didn't know it was you last night, they sure do now. The whole town is talking."

"Well, they have to talk about someone. So, what's with Flori? Should I come over?"

"No, she'll tell you when she's dried up. I'd say in about ten minutes."

He hung up.

Jake had been right. Ten minutes later, Flori called.

"Mabel," she cried. "You won't believe what I just found out. Do you know who Calvin took to the city with the retired people this morning?"

"The retired people?"

"Yes, you know the weekly trip? The Retirement Home? Have you forgotten already? They told me that I couldn't go because they were taking someone else. I thought they would take Erma because I suggested her to take your place. Well, she isn't going either. Calvin is taking some blond bimbo with him. A stranger, Mabel. The Home is allowing Calvin to take some woman with him who isn't even from around here." She started to sniff. "I'm so upset. How could they treat Erma and me this way?" She started to sob.

I waited. If Jake said she'd call when she dried up, she obviously hadn't waited long enough.

She was still sniffling but I took a chance and asked, "How did you find this out?"

"MJ phoned before they left. She was so upset. Everyone thought that Erma and I were coming. Mabel, I feel so helpless. What if something terrible happens to those old folks? I would never forgive myself."

"Flori, you don't have to forgive yourself for anything. You tried your best. What about Mr. Kinney? What's he thinking? Who is this woman anyway?"

"MJ said she came in and met everyone while they were having breakfast. She couldn't remember her name."

"What was she like? Was MJ afraid of her?"

"That's what hurts the most, Mabel. She said that she was a lovely person. Of course, all the men are happy because she's much prettier than Erma or me. And, a lot younger. Apparently, she has some degree. Something in the medical field. I guess Sam Kinney figures if something happens to any of those sweet old people that she'll be more help than us."

"How does Erma feel about it?"

"Calvin called her last night to tell her she wasn't needed anymore." A few more seconds of crying. "It was something that Erma was so looking forward to because life is getting hard with Murray. She needs a break."

"Murray's no better?"

"Worse. Erma thinks he's having a breakdown but he won't go to the doctor. She's at her wits end. Why don't you go to see her, Mabel? She could use some cheering up."

"Won't she be going to the book club tonight?"

"I hope so but she can't really pour out her heart to a room full of people. No, I think you should pay her a visit. Why don't you do that this afternoon? You don't have anything to do on Mondays anyway."

"Well, I could argue that point with you but I won't. Okay, I'll pop over when I've finished cleaning out the fridge and the freezer and washing the kitchen walls and repainting the bathroom. Oh, and did I mention swilling the hogs?"

Flori was laughing when I hung up and I hoped that would keep her going for the rest of the day. It was a dirty trick to play on those two women. If that had happened to me, I would be singing with relief but then, they weren't me.

It was slightly drizzling when I walked over to Erma's house. I saw Sammy lurching in the bushes, following me. It seemed that he was enjoying our newfound connection. Funny how Sammy got his name. I changed Phil's name to Phyl because 'he' turned out to be a 'her;' but Sammy, I named Samantha because Mutt swore it was a girl but 'she' turned out to be a 'he.' Most of the time, out of frustration I call any or all of them, 'Cat.'

Instead of taking the sidewalk to Irma's, I decided to walk along the beach. In Parson's Cove, we use the word 'beach' quite loosely. Along this side of the lake, it's about four feet wide with hard sand, dirt and gravel. It you drive three miles along the east shore you come to a beautiful long sandy beach with cottages and a privately owned campground. The drive is very picturesque as you travel along a narrow gravel road surrounded by forty-foot poplar, willow and cottonwood trees. If it weren't for this area, Parson's Cove wouldn't even be on a map.

The drizzle stopped and the wind came up. It was from the north and penetrated right through my shirt, sweater, and windbreaker. Everyone says that jeans are good for breaking the wind but I find that they're hot on hot days and cold on cold. They were definitely not keeping me warm at all. By the time I reached the carwash, I was shivering. Even when there was no sign of a crime anymore, it was still creepy. I stood for a few moments to envision Bernie stretched out in the lake with the blood stained water gently lapping against his lifeless body. I looked up at the back of the carwash. Someone had left the back door open again. Flori told me that no one was bringing cars here anymore and it would probably shut down. Personally, I never saw the need for one anyway. For goodness' sake, we live by a lake; drive up to it, fill a pail with water and throw it over your car.

Without thinking, I walked up to the building and looked in the back door. Someone had closed the front doors that faced Main Street so it was dark inside. This was the door where Melanie would've stood when she was looking for Bernie. I turned and looked toward the lake. How many feet was it to the water? Thirty?

Maybe forty, at the most? Had Bernie called out? If the air conditioner was on and the motor running, she would never have heard him. Is that what she'd planned? Was she playing a mind game with us?

In three minutes, I was walking up Erma and Murray's back yard. The tall grass made my shoes, socks and pant cuffs wet. This was a bad sign. Everyone knows Murray's plants are healthy and that he keeps his lawn looking manicured. I glanced over at their vegetable garden; it was hard to tell where the weeds ended and the tomato plants began.

Erma saw me through the kitchen window so met me at the patio doors.

"Come in, Mabel," she whispered. She walked into the kitchen and I followed.

"Why are we whispering?" I asked.

She motioned for me to sit down on one of her kitchen chairs. I watched as she tiptoed down the hallway and closed a door that I assumed was to a bedroom. She returned and collapsed in the chair across from me.

"Would you like a cup of coffee? It's only been sitting for about an hour."

"Just how I like it."

That wasn't true but I thought it would be easier to talk with a cup of something in my hand. She took down two mugs, filled them to the brim and brought them to the table.

"This is fine like this," I said. Somehow, I couldn't watch her clomp around the room anymore. I would chew the coffee if I had to.

She seemed grateful to sit down too.

"I don't know how much more I can take of this, Mabel," she said. "Murray's literally driving me crazy. He won't eat, won't sleep, and won't talk to me about anything. This is the first time he's slept in days and that's because I got some pills from Dr. Fritz. He told me to crush them and put them in his drinks. I put three in his last cup of tea. I hope I won't kill him."

"You mean it's still about Bernie? Or, is it his old dog?"

She shook her head. "I don't know. Doc Fritz thinks he was heading for some sort of meltdown and this aggravated it. You know, kind of like the straw that broke the camel's back. He says to be patient and he'll be okay in time." She looked up at me. There were tears in her eyes. "My patience is running out, Mabel. I'm afraid that one of these days, I might pick up a brick. Know what I mean?"

"Erma, there's no way you would ever do that. By the way, are you going to the book club tonight?"

"Nah, I haven't even opened the book we were supposed to read. What's the point?"

"The point is you get out of the house and away from Murray. And, away from your bricks."

This brought a slight smile to her lips. She was a pretty woman when she smiled.

"Maybe you're right. I should go."

"Give Flori a call. I know that she'd love to go with you. By the way, sorry to hear about your trip to the city. I don't know what Sam Kinney is thinking, sending a stranger with those poor people from the Home."

She shrugged. "I know Flori was counting on it but I think I would've been worrying all the time about Murray so it's probably for the best." She took a big gulp of coffee and made a face. "Man, this is awful coffee." She looked over at my cup, which was still almost full. "Let me make some fresh, Mabel. I'd really appreciate it if you'd stay awhile and visit."

"Sure," I said. "Flori reminded me this morning that I really didn't have much to do on Mondays so it's nice to have someone to visit with." I handed her my cup and she poured the black liquid down the drain. While she was making a fresh pot, I looked around her kitchen. I knew after they retired, Erma looked after the inside of the house and Murray kept up the yard. It's easy to see when either someone is depressed or going through hard times because their work suffers. The last time I'd been here, Erma's countertop and table had been immaculately clean and tidy. Now, several different items cluttered the tabletop and there was barely an inch of counter showing. One item on the table caught my attention: a red plastic bowl filled with bottles of prescription drugs. Underneath them was a small packet filled with a white substance.

"Do you and Murray take all these pills?" I asked.

She clicked on the coffee maker and sat down before answering.

"Well," she said. "Dr. Fritz has Murray on two kinds of pills for depression and anxiety. I have hypertension so I have two medications for that." She showed me the bottles. "I've already crushed some of Murray's pills and put them into this plastic wrap. This is what I put in his tea."

"I wonder why he didn't put his name on Murray's pills. Did you notice that, Erma? Look, your prescription is filled out properly but Murray's isn't."

She turned slightly pink. "I know it's silly but I asked him not to. I've been telling Murray that they're vitamins."

That made a lot of sense. Some women seem to know how to handle difficult situations. I don't think I would be so intuitive. It still seemed strange to me how Murray was reacting to this. Why was he having a breakdown? Did he know who killed Bernie?

I reached for my fresh cup of coffee. My fingers suddenly felt cold and shaky. How many Parsons' Cove people were involved in this? How many of my neighbors were covering up for each other?

Reg would need to know. It would be easier for him to talk to Murray. As long as Erma hadn't put too many crushed pills in his tea.

Chapter Thirty Five

Prunella was home from the hospital so I thought I might as well make a quick stop at her place. After all, she would probably want to thank me in person for saving her life.

I didn't see the police car parked in her driveway until I was almost in front of the house. Did I dare take the chance and knock? Really, what did I have to lose? The worst they could do was tell me that I couldn't see Prunella.

I went round to the back door. The inside door was open so I could see into the kitchen through the screen door. There was no one there but I could hear mumbled talking from somewhere else in the house. I opened the door gently and stepped inside to have a quick look around.

Not much had changed. The glasses on the table were gone, of course. It looked as though someone had attempted to clean up. I couldn't help but wonder whose prints were on those glasses. Questions were piling on top of questions. Who hit Prunella on the head with the frying pan? Why wouldn't she admit someone hit her? Whom was she protecting? Did someone put drugs in her rum and coke or was she taking them herself? Why was there a wad of money and a packet of some unknown substance in her dresser drawer and who gave it to her?

The closer I got inside the room, the clearer the voices became. It was definitely two women. One was Prunella and since the other must be with the police force, it had to be the female cop that I'd seen before. I felt a little braver knowing that and took a couple of steps across the kitchen. There was a lull in the conversation so I stood still, not even breathing. When they started up again, I could hear every word.

"Prunella, you have to let us help you." The unknown woman said. "You know very well your life is in danger if you stay here by yourself. Whoever did this to you will come back."

Prunella's voice was softer and not so strong. "I told you, Officer, I'll be fine. I can look after myself. You wanted to know about Melanie and Bernie and I've told you that I couldn't hear too clearly. It was nothing. I wish I'd never bothered. Married people fight all the time. I should've minded my own business."

"That's the problem. You first said that you could hear everything very clearly, now you're saying you didn't. Why did you change your statement, Prunella? Someone almost killed you. Why are you trying to cover it up? What about the money and the drugs, Prunella? There was over a thousand dollars in that pouch. You can't remember where it came from?"

Now, my ears really perked up.

"Officer, I told you before that I forgot I had the money there. I put it there a while ago for safekeeping. That's all. It's my money and I can do with it what I want."

No one spoke for several moments and I started to panic but then the police officer spoke.

"All right, now you say it's your money. Why did you tell us before that it wasn't? That you had no idea where it came from? Do you think perhaps someone knew that you had money hidden and came for it but when you wouldn't tell them where it was, they hit you on the head and left you for dead?"

"No, I told you no one hit me on the head. I just got dizzy and fell. I don't know why you never found any blood and I don't remember how I got to my bed. No one knew that I had any money hidden away. Why don't you just leave me alone?"

"All right, Prunella, but there are still many unanswered questions. Be prepared for questioning from more cops. We're going to get down to the bottom of this. If someone threatened you in any way, we can protect you. You know that, don't you?"

I don't know how Prunella replied because I heard the bedsprings squeak and I quickly and quietly made my exit. The police knew no more than what I did - at least, when it came to Prunella.

I wasn't inside my house more than five minutes when the phone rang. It was May.

"Mabel," she said. "I'm sorry I didn't call sooner. I think there's something you might find interesting. Do you have a minute?"

"Of course, I do. I'm curious."

"Well, it might not be all that important but I found it to be odd so I did a little sneaking around. You know, when Prunella was in here? Well, she had a visitor every day. I was surprised but then, what do I know? You see many strange things after working in the hospital for all these years. What struck me as odd was that this visitor always visited Prunella when she was alone. I checked and when she had someone in her room, he would not go in; in fact, he would disappear."

"May, I'm all ears. Who was it?"

"It was Melanie's brother, Steve. Now, why would he be visiting Prunella? I've never known them to be friends. I don't think any of Melanie's family bothers with Prunella, do they?"

"Not that I know of. You didn't happen to hear anything, did you?"

"Well, matter of fact, I did. I was very discreet though, Mabel. You know I could get into trouble. Although, who would get upset with a little old lady who couldn't remember which floor she was on, right?"

"Right. You're amazing, May."

"I don't know if it's important but anyway, I heard Steve telling Prunella that she'd better keep her mouth shut. Which is very suspicious right there, right? Then, I heard him say something about being involved whether she liked it or not because he would make sure of it. He mumbled something about planting something. Do you have any idea what that means?"

"I have a fair idea. Did he say anything about being at her place?"

"Sorry, Mabel. That's all I heard. A nurse came along and I had to rush back to my desk. She gave me a funny look and asked what I was doing up there so I didn't try going up again."

"What did you tell her? You know, why you were up there?"

"I told her I was passing on a phone message which makes no sense because there's a phone in every room but she seemed satisfied with the answer. If I hear anything more about Prunella or the murder, I'll make sure to pass it on."

"Thank you so much, May. I'm going to give Reg a call and let him know. The pieces are falling into place."

"You know who killed Bernie?"

I sighed. "That I don't know and it's getting quite frustrating. Sometimes, it takes awhile but I have a gut feeling that we're getting closer."

"Well, I'm pulling for you, Mabel. I hope you and Reg solve the case. I'll be glad when all those city cops are out of town. Besides, I'm tired of Scully pulling me over every time I forget to put on my signal lights. Amy

Hunter told me Jim sits in front of her place making sure everyone slows down for the kids. She said she appreciates that but not when he makes all the mothers walk down to the corner to cross. What's the matter with those two anyway?"

I had to laugh. "I guess they have to do something. It keeps them out of trouble."

Ten minutes after I called and left a message, Reg was at the door.

"What do you think, Mabel?" He sat across from me at the kitchen table.

"For one thing, Reg, I think Steve must be the one who hit Prunella on the head. Why else would he be visiting her every day in the hospital? And, why would he make sure he went in when no one else was there? May said he told Prunella to keep her mouth shut, which sounds threatening to me. Also, he told her that she was involved whether she liked it or not and that he'd planted something. What I'd like to know is - involved in what and what did he plant? Was it the money and drugs in her bedroom and if he did, why?"

"You might be on to something, Mabel. By the way, the drugs we found in Calvin's hubcaps were nothing but crushed pills for diabetics. Now, why would someone hide a legitimate drug?"

I shook my head. It didn't make any sense at all. "Speaking of drugs, when I was at Erma's place, she showed me the pills that she gives to Murray. She crushes them up and puts them in his tea. Fritzy didn't put his name on the pill bottles so Erma could tell Murray that they were vitamins. I guess otherwise he wouldn't take them."

Reg stood up. "Poor Murray. I hope he snaps out of this soon. You know what, Mabel, I'm beginning to wonder if he doesn't know who killed Bernie."

"What?"

"Well, why else would he be acting like this? Or, what about Murray? What if he's the one who hit Bernie on the head? It happened right behind his house. It could've been an accident."

"Are you serious? I can't imagine Murray killing anyone. If it was an accident, I'm sure he would've come forward. Don't you think so?"

He shook his head. "I don't know. We have to think of everyone, Mabel. Everyone is a suspect. You know this dead fish smell? I think it was to cover up the smell of drugs so that if the cops pulled them over, the dogs couldn't smell anything. What do you think?"

I was trying not to get too excited. "That very thought crossed my mind too. About the fish smell but not Murray. I'm sure Murray couldn't have killed Bernie. But, Reg, if they were selling drugs why did the packet we took have crushed diabetic pills in it? Where were the illegal drugs?"

"Because, now that I think of it, I took the only loose packet. All the others were wrapped up with cellophane."

"So, the dogs that are trained to sniff out cocaine wouldn't bother with the dead fish smell but boy, my cat sure would! And, I wonder about Biscuit. You should ask Erma if their old dog loved to eat fish. Remember Murray used to go fishing with Bernie and the dog went with them in the boat. I'm still thinking that maybe that's why Biscuit met his waterloo. Maybe he was doing the same thing as Sammy but instead of kicking him, Calvin threw a brick. Reg, those people renting Krueger's house must be buying up the drugs. Remember I saw Calvin and Scooter over there. What if they were getting back into the car and there was Biscuit, sniffing the hubcaps and going crazy? Or, attacking Calvin trying to rip his boots off. "

Excitement shone in Reg's eyes. "There's a pile of old bricks in the empty lot beside the house." He rubbed his hands together. "I'll find out about Biscuit and his love for fish but first, I'm going to check out those bricks. Maybe I'll drop in and visit your friends living behind you. What did you say the guy's name was?"

"Jeff. I think he told me his wife's name but I can't remember. All I know is that she's very blond."

"Blond? I bet I know who she is. Is she the woman Calvin is taking on the bus with him to the city? Sam Kinney said she was blond. Calvin showed up at Sam's office with her and with a three-page resume. Said she had all these degrees in psychology and experience working in care homes."

"You mean he's willing to hire some blond stranger and pay her while he could get Flori for free?"

"Oh no, he's not paying her. She's volunteering. Wanting to help out while she's vacationing here. Told him that this is how she always spends her summers – helping out the less fortunate."

"So, she really has all those degrees?"

He shrugged. "Sam hadn't checked her out yet when I last saw him. He said all the seniors seemed to be taken with her though so he wasn't too concerned."

"You know what? People in small towns are way too trusting. What's the matter with us anyway? We hire strangers without a blink of the eye. Someday, someone in Parson's Cove will end up murdered; that's what will happen."

Reg smiled but it was a sad smile. "We have someone murdered, Mabel, and I'm betting it wasn't a stranger who did the killing."

For a moment, I couldn't think of anything to say. He was right. Why was I worrying about strangers when there was probably a respected citizen walking around who'd hit Bernie over the head and killed him.

"It makes me shudder to think of that. Well, maybe we haven't found the killer but I think we've discovered something else, Reg. This has to be a drug ring. Calvin and Scooter are obviously bringing drugs into Parson's Cove. They're hiding them in the soles of shoes that Scooter is claiming to repair and also behind the hubcaps in the taxi. If the cops ever stop them doing a random search for drugs, they don't worry because the dogs won't smell them."

"So how does Bernie fit into all of this, Mabel? It has to somehow be tied into that murder."

"I wonder if Bernie was dealing. Melanie said he was acting strange. Someone must've double crossed him."

"Or, he double crossed someone."

"What can I do, Reg? I can't sit and do nothing."

"You've got the house behind you to watch. Let's see what kind of action is going on there."

He walked over to the window and looked out. "There's a few places in your yard where you can sit and not be seen. Why don't you sit outside and do some reading or something?"

"All right but it seems pretty quiet over there right now. I wonder what they do all day."

Reg winked. "Maybe you could find out."

That was the first time in history that Reg suggested something like that so I certainly wasn't going to dismiss it. He's usually telling me to mind my own business.

Chapter Thirty Six

It isn't much fun standing at your kitchen window staring at your neighbor's house or hiding behind a lilac bush waiting for something to happen. Sometimes a person has to take action. I pulled a bag of frozen apple muffins out of my freezer, popped them in the microwave and headed for Krueger's house. The gate hadn't been pried open all summer so it took a few minutes to untangle some of the vines. I've let them grow so I don't have to see my neighbor's back yard. Our one and only real estate company is supposed to keep the grass cut and the hedges trimmed but the boys they send over don't do much of a job.

I managed to yank the gate open and then gingerly make my way to the back door. It seemed to be worse this summer than most. Once you allow thistles to start multiplying, you're in for trouble. As soon as I returned home, I was going to give Shirley, at BuyRHomes, a call. If Old Man Krueger could see how his house and yard looked now, he'd die all over again.

Before I reached the step, Jeff opened the door. He opened it, stepped out, and then closed it. Obviously, he was not inviting me in for tea.

"Well, I see my neighbor has come calling," he said. "Sorry, I'm just heading out."

"Oh, that's okay. I brought some fresh muffins over. I'm sorry I haven't been over earlier to meet your wife. How is she enjoying our little town? I'm sure it must be quite boring for her. Or, does she like fishing?" I handed the bag of muffins to him.

He took the brown paper bag. "This is very kind of you. Actually, my wife really likes it here. She's not much for fishing but she always finds something to do." He smiled and turned to the door. "Thanks again. I'm sure we'll enjoy these."

Before he could disappear back into the house, I said, "I hear your wife loves doing volunteer work. Someone said she's going to work at the Parson's Cove Seniors' Home. I think that's so wonderful. There aren't too many nowadays who want to put themselves out for others. Don't you find that?" I shook my head. "I don't know. The world is changing so much. We had a murder in town here not long ago and now people have started locking their doors. It isn't the same as it used to be." I gave him a big smile. "Tell your wife that everyone in Parson's Cove would like to thank her for helping us out."

Jeff didn't seem to know what to say so I continued, "I feel silly saying this but I don't even know your wife's name. I'm sure you mentioned it before but I'm so forgetful. What was it again?"

"Jennifer. Her name's Jennifer. I'll tell her what you said, Mabel."

"Jennifer. That's really cute: Jeff and Jennifer. Oh, I guess she's gone on the bus with Calvin now, isn't she? My friend, Flori, and I went a week or so ago. I have to say, I'm very thankful for Jennifer taking over. It takes a special kind of person to get along with all those oldies. Not that they aren't nice, mind you; I just find it very tiring. I'm sure your wife will make out fine though. She's young and has more energy."

He waved the bag. "Once again, thanks for these, Mabel. Sorry but I have to rush away."

Before I could ask him where he was going, he disappeared into the house. I stood for a few minutes on the step, thinking he might reappear but when I heard him talking on the phone, I headed back home. If I could've heard what he was saying, I might have lingered for another minute or so.

I went back inside and watched through the kitchen window. About ten minutes later, Jeff came out. I moved away from the window in case he was watching. When I looked again, he was disappearing around the corner.

The afternoon was getting away on me. Calvin would be returning from the city soon. How much time did I have? A half hour to an hour at the most.

First of all, I did knock. Very loudly. Then, to make sure, I opened the door and yelled.

"Jeff? Jennifer? Are you here?" Then, more loudly, in case someone was lurking anywhere, I yelled out again, "Just checking to see if everyone is okay. Shirley wanted me to check on you." Okay, so that was a blatant lie but if I needed to save my hide, it would be worth it.

There was no answer. The only sound was the hum of the old refrigerator. It was as old as the house almost and I remembered it from a few previous break-ins. (Me breaking in, that is.)

I stepped in and closed the door. The kitchen looked the same as it had when Mr. Krueger built the house. Very sad. At least, I've installed new cupboards and windows within the last twenty years. The Krueger house, sat frozen in time. A fleeting feeling of sadness and nostalgia passed through me. It had to be fleeting because I had very little time to do what I needed to do.

I did a quick survey of the kitchen. There were no obvious signs of drugs anywhere. I opened the cupboards, pulled out the drawers and checked the fridge. All I found were dishes, cutlery and food. Next, I tackled the upstairs. There were two bedrooms and a bathroom. Where does a person look for illegal drugs? I lifted the mattresses, looked under the beds and checked all the drawers. There were less places to search in the bathroom; and like the bedrooms, I came up empty.

One place left to investigate - the basement. This is not my favorite spot. A few years' back, I happened upon a dead body down there. About a year later, I hid down there, fearing for my life. As I descended the stairs, it did not bring back any happy memories.

It was as messy and musty smelling as I remembered. In fact, it looked the same as it had about a year ago, except for three boxes piled one on top of the other, sitting at the bottom of the steps. It was a good place to start my search because if I found what I was looking for, I wouldn't have to go into any dark creepy corners.

My only problem was the duck tape. How could I rip off the tape and sneak a look without Jeff knowing?

I needn't have worried. There was a loud rap on the kitchen door; then, another knock - louder than the first. The door opened and someone called out Jeff's name. He called three times, each time louder than the time before.

I eased myself back into a dark creepy corner behind the steps.

Much to my dismay, whoever was up there was not leaving. In fact, he walked directly down the creaky wooden stairs. He stopped at the boxes. If he'd turned his head and peered through the steps, he would've looked right into my eyes. My back was up against the cement wall so I wasn't going anywhere. All I had going for me was luck and that wasn't too reassuring.

I could see who it was, however, and that made me somewhat apprehensive. Not that I'd ever thought of Scooter as a killer but I wasn't really trusting that many people in Parson's Cove anymore. I became even more concerned when I saw him yank up his pant leg and whip out a deadly looking hunting knife that he had strapped to his leg. He pulled it out and sliced the duck tape in one swift easy motion. Obviously, he was in a hurry to get into that box because he dropped the knife on the floor and ripped open the flaps.

I have no idea what expression he had on his face because my eyes were where his were – on the contents of that box. He reached his hand in and I held my breath. Slowly he removed one plastic bag after another and set them on the floor. After he'd removed them all (I would say there were about twenty bags), he put them back. That is, all of them but two. Those two, he stuffed into his jacket pockets. Then, he carefully put the box that he'd opened at the bottom of the pile. That's how intelligent Scooter is.

At this point, both of my feet were beginning to tingle so I was hoping he'd escape with those bags before I collapsed on the floor. That, however, appeared to be the least of my worries.

Someone was banging on the door. Three callers in one afternoon. Several loud raps and then, "Open up. Police!"

Scooter stood frozen in his tracks; fear, shock and panic engraved on his face.

The kitchen door suddenly burst open with such force that the house shuddered. By the sounds of the footsteps above, there must have been dozens of cops. I'm not sure if they were taking turns yelling, 'police' but it seemed that they were.

Scooter hadn't moved. He looked up to the top of the stairs and as his eyes lowered, they rested right on mine. Neither one of us moved. He stared at me and I stared back. Unfortunately, his brain went into gear before mine did. In one swift move, he picked up his knife, dashed around the staircase and grabbed me by the arm. Perhaps if both my feet hadn't been asleep, I could've tried to escape. As it was, I simply sank to the cement floor forcing Scooter to hold me up while pointing his hunting knife at my neck.

"Ow," I yelled. "What do you think you're doing?"

"What do you *think* I'm doing? Stand up and you won't get hurt."

"I can't stand up; my feet are dead. I can't move them."

"You'd better move them," he hissed in my ear, "Or your feet won't be the only thing that's dead."

"Oh, you'll use your knife this time? Can't find a brick?"

I guess some of the cops stopped yelling upstairs long enough to hear us and yelled down from the top of the stairs, "Okay, down there, come up with your hands in front so we can see them."

"Mabel," Scooter said, very quietly, "I want you to walk in front of me. Put your hands up but remember I'll be right behind you with a knife in your back. Got that?"

"I got that but I think you're going about this whole thing in the wrong way."

"Oh well, pardon me, how should I be going about it?"

Another voice bellowed from above, "Did you hear me down there? Get up here and hold your hands up where I can see them."

I'd recognize that bellow anywhere. "It's okay, Captain Maxymowich. This is Mabel Wickles down here. Scooter and I will be up in a minute."

Scooter's hand dropped down.

"Oh boy, now why did you have to go and do that?" he said. "Don't you know I could kill you if I wanted to? What's the matter with you anyway?"

"What's the matter with me? Don't you know you're in big enough trouble? If those are your drugs down here, then you'll be carted off to jail for who knows how long. But, if you're only breaking and entering, of which I'm also guilty, then you might not even go to jail. Don't you even think before you do things?"

"Are you all right down there, Mabel?" Maxymowich yelled.

"I'm okay. We're on our way up now. Scooter has a knife but I'm sure he isn't going to use it on me."

I once again had feeling in my feet and as I started up the stairs, I could hear Scooter muttering, "Stupid old biddy. Stupid woman. Shoulda killed her when I had the chance."

By the time I'd reached the third rung, I looked up. Five guns stared me in the face. The Captain was standing in the center of the doorway, his gun drawn as if nothing in the human realm could harm him. To his left, on his knees, was a tough looking bald cop who looked like he could pull the trigger and not even break a sweat. Above him, was the female cop, both hands holding the gun straight out in front of her and kindly pointing it right at me. On the other side of the door were two more cops in the same formation. No one was smiling so I knew this was no joke. I raised my arms and ascended the steps. This is not as easy as it sounds, especially if you're anticipating a knife being hurled into your back at any time.

Chapter Thirty Seven

"Are you crazy, Mabel?" Reg said. "I asked you to watch the house, not break and enter it." He rolled his eyes and shook his head. He'd been pacing the floor for the past ten minutes.

"Would you please sit down? You're driving me crazy. Every time I look up to say something, you're at the other end of the room."

"And, what do you have to say? You can make up every excuse in the book to me but what the heck are you going to tell Maxymowich?" He finally pulled out one of my kitchen chairs and sat down. With a big sigh, of course. He leaned over and stared at me. "So, Mabel? What are you going to tell him? I think it's amazing that he sent you home and didn't cuff you."

"Oh come off it, Reg. Maxymowich knows that I'm not a drug runner or whatever they're called. Also, since I'm the one whose back was in the most danger of being speared, I don't think he was too concerned. Besides, there was a bag of my fresh muffins sitting on the table so I can clearly explain my reason for being there."

"Ha! You were taking the long way home through the basement? Come on, you know very well you can't just walk into people's homes and snoop around. Even cops need a search warrant."

"That's right, Reg. Cops need a permit but since I'm not a cop, I can just walk in. Especially if I suspect something illegal is going on. It's my duty to protect my neighbors. What kind of person would I be if I didn't? Haven't you heard of a citizen's arrest?"

I was waiting for a burst of cuss words but instead Sheriff Smee started laughing so hard, I thought he was going to fall off his chair.

"Okay, Reg. What's so darn funny? One minute you're mad at me and the next you think I'm a big joke, is that it?"

The sheriff pulled a red cotton handkerchief out of his back pocket and wiped his eyes. Beth had obviously missed this hankie when she did her Monday wash.

"No, I don't think you're a joke at all. I think you could talk your way out of anything." He stood up, with a smirk still on his face. "Well, I won't worry about you, Mabel. Give me a call in the morning and let me know how you make out. In fact, try to get as much information out of the Captain as you can." He started chuckling again.

Before he reached the door, he turned and said, "By the way, that pile of bricks in the yard next to Krueger's? That pile's been sitting there for years and there was obviously one brick missing. It's the one that someone used to hit Biscuit and Bernie on the head. And, Murray? I tried to talk to him but he was so drugged and confused, all he could talk about was God and that if Melanie was found guilty, God would look after her."

I imagine that Erma was rethinking how many crushed pills she should put in Murray's tea.

I didn't have to wait too long for Maxymowich to show up. He knocked on the door about two hours later. I held it open and he sauntered into the kitchen. He pulled out a chair and slumped into it as if he did this sort of thing on a regular basis.

After running his fingers through his white hair several times he said, "Mabel, I could sure use a cup of coffee and a nice fresh muffin. Strawberry, if you have it."

"Captain," I said. "This is Mabel Wickles' restaurant. It will take only a few minutes. However, before I start brewing fresh coffee, I'd like to know if I'm being charged with any crime; after all, I was in someone's home uninvited."

"Really?" he said. "I didn't realize that. I've always been under the impression that, as a good neighbor, you always keep your eye on Miss Krueger's house." He raised his eyebrows. "Or, was I mistaken?"

"Absolutely not. In fact, I just finished telling Sheriff Smee the exact same thing." I gave him my best smile. He had no idea how much better my stomach felt. "If you'd like you could relax in the living room and I'll bring the coffee in as soon as it's ready."

He looked around my kitchen as if that would help make up his mind. His eyes rested on the five cats who were sitting in a row, staring up at him. "I think I'll stay here. Those cats might attack me without you close by." Then, smiling, he said, "Besides, you have a very comfortable kitchen, Mabel."

I didn't have the heart to tell him that he made me uncomfortable.

"Are you curious about the drug bust we made? Or, should I say the one that you helped us make?" he asked.

"Helped you?" I sat down. "I didn't realize anyone from the police department was aware of anything I was doing."

"Oh, trust me, Mabel; we're always aware of what you're doing." Another attractive smile.

"I guess that should be reassuring to me." I smiled my best smile in return. "So, Scooter was stealing drugs from Jeff?"

He nodded. "How about you keep working on that coffee? Can I talk to you while you're doing that?"

My face felt slightly warmer than normal. "Of course," I said. "Would you like to try my new apple muffins?" Without waiting for a reply, I went into my pantry and pulled out one bag of strawberry and one bag of apple muffins. There were a dozen in each bag so I knew I'd be sharing muffins with a few people for the next day or so.

After I'd popped two muffins into the microwave and while I was spooning coffee into the filter, he said, "I've learned not to tell you to stop being your curious self, Mabel; however, there are a few things you don't have to worry about anymore. For example, there's no need for you to check out anyone's work boots. Nor is it necessary to send your cats to smell anyone's tires."

"Oh, you knew about that?"

He nodded. His face was serious but his eyes weren't. "Yes, and it was smart to check it out but you really should've come to me. It's much wiser to work along with the police, Mabel. I thought maybe you would know that by now."

The muffins were ready so I put them on a plate and set them on the table. I opened the fridge and brought out the butter.

"I'm sorry; the butter is as hard as rock but if you put it on while your muffins are hot, you'll be okay."

I watched as he cut both muffins in half and added a good tablespoon slab of butter to each one. The butter slowly melted on top and oozed over the sides. As soon as he was gone and I could relax, I was going to have one myself.

Meanwhile, there was something I wanted Mr. Maxymowich to understand. "Of course, Captain, you realize that I was with my local sheriff at the time. However, I do appreciate the fact that everyone needs help now and again. I always feel that there are places I can go or people that I can talk to who won't ever talk to you. Some would even talk to Reg before they would talk to a city cop." I poured his coffee and set it down in front of him. I knew he drank his black so I went to the fridge to get some milk for mine. I brought my cup to the table and sat across from him.

He picked up his cup, took a sip and literally smacked his lips. Without saying anything more, I watched as he carefully lifted his butter and cholesterol-laden muffin and started to eat. He obviously didn't want to be disturbed so I drank my coffee in silence.

After several minutes, he spoke, "You're quite right, Mabel. No one wants to share things with a stranger. I'll share a few things with you though." He picked up a napkin and wiped some butter off his chin. "I guess we're not considered strangers anymore, are we?" Not waiting for an answer, he continued, "Jeff Keeler and Jennifer Wilson store most of their drugs in an old house not far from Parson's Cove. It's by the lake and hidden back in the woods. We've been watching them for quite some time. From there, they distribute their drugs. They didn't want anyone finding out where it was so they rented the house behind yours."

"You mean they're not husband and wife?"

He shook his head. "Not in God's eyes, no. I think they like to think of themselves as another Bonnie and Clyde."

"You know she's volunteering for the seniors' home, don't you?"

"Yes, I do. As you and your cat know, Calvin was transporting drugs from the city to here. Jennifer and Jeff were expanding their little business. Scooter was moving drugs in the soles of shoes, as you and your cat also know. They'd bring the drugs to Jeff and he'd distribute them."

"Do you know what that awful smell was? It smelled like dead fish. It drove my cat crazy. I think it was just the paper bag that the drugs were in that smelled like that though."

"You're right. They found a drug called metformin. It's a legitimate drug for diabetes but most people refuse to take it because it smells so bad. They thought that if the cops ever stopped them on the highway and there were dogs, they wouldn't be caught. And, they always made sure one bottle of metformin was in the hubcap or a few pills in the shoes. Chances were that the cops would pick those pills to test."

"That's exactly what happened. Reg grabbed the one loose packet and it was the diabetes drug. What about at Scooter's house though? You didn't find any real drugs there?"

"We found quite a few bottles of metformin at Scooter's place, that's all. Jeff had cleared everything out and had taken some to the cabin and some to Krueger's house." He laughed. "But who knew that it would be a cat that would catch them?"

"I guess in a way it was Sammy who played a part in catching those dealers, wasn't it? But, Captain, wouldn't it be ironic if it was Biscuit, Murray's dog, who also started sniffing the tires or the shoes? I'm wondering if that isn't why someone killed him."

The Captain's eyes widened. "You might have something there, Mabel."

"I mean, it would be either Scooter or Calvin, wouldn't it?"

"It could've been."

"But who were buying the drugs? That's what I can't figure out. I know I'm not out cruising the streets at night but I really haven't heard of any drug problems and neither has Reg."

"No, you wouldn't. Most of the drugs aren't out in the streets, Mabel. At least, not these drugs. They're being sold within the confines of a secure place. Some drug dealers concentrate on kids because they're vulnerable and some take advantage of another defenseless group."

"Are you trying to tell me that Jeff and Jennifer are selling drugs to the people in the retirement home?"

"Well, they were selling them to the new manager."

"Sam Kinney? They were selling drugs to Sam Kinney? I don't believe it."

"Believe it. He was giving small doses to some of the more wealthy residents until they got hooked and then he started charging."

"What kind of drugs? I don't know much about using drugs but if they were all high on cocaine wouldn't some of the staff know it?"

"Not cocaine. It was methamphetamine. It makes a person feel good, gives them energy and in some cases makes them, let's say, a bit frisky."

"You're kidding. Well, I'm pretty sure I know one person who's hooked on it – Sam Dudley. I thought I was the only one that he chased but some of the women in the Home said he was getting quite aggressive with his wandering hands."

"Another problem is that it's highly addictive."

"What's going to happen to all those drugged old people?"

"It will take awhile to wean them off of it. It might take up to six months for some of them. We've already spoken to family members."

"Where are all the crooks now?"

"They're all being escorted back to the city where they'll be held until there's a bail hearing. Next week sometime, I expect."

"So, what crooks are we talking about here?"

"Obviously, Jeff and Jennifer. Also, Sam Kinney. I doubt they will see the light of day for some time. Scooter and Calvin will probably return but could end up serving some time. Depends on the judge, I guess. Neither one has a criminal record so the court might go easy on them."

"When you started, you said you would tell me all that you know. What don't you know?"

"Who killed Bernie Bernstein."

"Aw yes, Bernie. Somehow, in all this other mess, we've forgotten the real crime. Since Bernie seemed to be bringing drugs in his car too, who do you think killed him? Calvin or Scooter? If they're sent back to Parson's Cove that means a killer has been let on the loose."

"Well, both men swear they didn't have anything to do with his murder and we don't have any proof. In fact, both men have an alibi for the time that Bernie was killed."

"Do you really think it was Melanie then?"

Captain Maxymowich drained his cup and stood up. "She did confess to it and Prunella heard them arguing. Melanie did threaten to kill him."

"But you don't believe that, do you? I would believe her brother did it before I'd believe that she did. By the way, did you know that her brother spent quite a bit of time visiting Prunella in the hospital? May West said that she heard Steve threaten her. Have you checked into that?"

"We spoke with May yesterday. We need a reason and a confession from Steve. So far, he's been very uncooperative."

"So what does Prunella say?"

"She says Steve is a good friend and has never threatened her in any way."

"Well, not a big surprise there. Prunella seems to say whatever anyone tells her to say. I'm shocked she even said anything when she saw Bernie and Melanie arguing. Although I bet she wouldn't have if Esther hadn't told her she had to. I just wish we could find whoever killed Bernie. And, I don't mean accepting Melanie's confession. By the way, do you know if Bernie was really into selling drugs or what was the deal with him?"

"Bernie got involved quite by accident. Calvin and Scooter aren't giving too much information about him but that's because both of them are high on the suspect list."

"You mean it started when he got the wrong shoes from Scooter?"

The Captain nodded. "Yeah, he figured he was onto something - something where he could cash in and make some money. Scooter said Bernie told him that if they didn't let him in on the operation that he'd go to the cops."

"Doesn't that pretty much prove that either Calvin or Scooter killed him?"

He shrugged. "It would except for the fact that both of the men have alibis. There's no way they could've been two places at once."

"What about Jeff? Or, Jennifer, for that matter?"

He shook his head. "We've checked them out too. Jennifer was in the city where, believe it or not, she worked in a care home for the elderly. Jeff was sitting in Main Street Café most of the afternoon and there were several people who saw him."

I stared at him. "Jennifer looks after elderly people? I sure hope you're checking that place out."

He smiled. "As we speak."

"This whole thing is so baffling. Parson's Cove is suffering because of it too. We used to trust all our neighbors. Now, we're all paranoid that there's a killer wandering the streets."

"I know how you feel, Mabel, and Sheriff Smee and his deputies will be increasing their patrolling time. You'll see them out on the streets a lot more until this person is found."

"You mean you're leaving and not coming back?"

"Oh, I'll be in touch with Reg constantly and we'll be checking out other people of interest. The thing is, Bernie could've had contact with drug dealers in the city. We want to find out exactly how involved he was getting and how many enemies he really did have out there."

"This is getting to be too complicated. Would you like another cup of coffee?"

"No, thanks, but if you don't mind, I wouldn't mind having a muffin 'to go.'"

"I don't mind at all. I'll put one in a bag for you."

He smiled – one of his rare 'show all your teeth' smiles, and said, "I guess I was thinking more along the lines of 'one bag of muffins to go.'"

Who can resist Captain Marlow Maxymowich's smile? I handed both bags to him and said, "Enjoy them. If you have to come back to Parson's Cove again, I'll make sure to have more fresh muffins to go."

It had been a long day so after Maxymowich left, I changed into my pajamas, brushed my teeth, made a small gin and tonic and went to bed.

I settled in for the night. The cats were snuggled into their usual spots, and I was half way through my lovely nightcap when I heard someone opening the back door. Flori is the only person who has a key.

"Mabel, where are you?" she screamed. "Answer me right now. Are you all right?"

Before I had time to rush to the bathroom and pour my drink down the sink, Flori was pounding up the stairs. All I could do was set my glass on the floor as far under the bed as I could reach. I straightened up when she came puffing into my room. Her hair was sticking out in every direction and she was wearing her nightgown under a pink housecoat.

"Flori, what on earth are you doing here at this time of night? Why didn't you phone? You don't even have any makeup on."

"I just heard now. Probably everyone in Parson's Cove knows but no one told me. And you, Mabel Wickles, didn't even let me know. As soon as Jake came home and told me, I ran straight over here." She rushed over to the bed and plunked down beside me, putting her arm around me. With her face about an inch away from mine, she said, "What's that smell?"

She sniffed the air. "Yes, there's a definite smell coming from you. Were you in the gin again, Mabel?"

I'd held my breath when she was near me for as long as I could and when I let out all the pent up air, she screwed up her face and said, "Phew. That's the foulest smelling breath I've ever smelled."

"Flori," I said. "Did you want to hear about my harrowing near death experience or do want to continue smelling my breath?"

"All right, I want to hear but we'll talk about the other before I leave." She grabbed my hand and held on. "Please, tell me it isn't true that Scooter shoved a knife into your throat."

As if the reality of it just sank in, she lifted her hand and pushed up my chin to check for scars. Or, knowing Flori, maybe dried blood.

"I can't see anything," she said. "So, did he poke your neck with his knife or not?"

"Well, not really. I think he tried to but my feet were asleep so he had to hold me up and I guess it's kind of hard to slit someone's throat and hold them up at the same time."

Flori's color changed from white to pink and then back to white. "He tried to slit your throat?"

"No, Flori. You know Scooter; he's a big talker. I was a little nervous when he made me go up the stairs and said he'd have the knife in my back though."

"Oh my lord, what did you do?"

"There really wasn't much to worry about. Five cops were at the top of the stairs with guns pointed down at us. If Scooter would've knifed me, five guns would have gone off and Scooter would be plastered all over Krueger's basement walls."

"Oh Mabel, what a dreadful thing to say. How can you be so blasé about the whole thing? He could've killed you. But what I can't understand is, why were you in Krueger's house in the first place? And, what on earth were you doing in the basement? Did Scooter force you to go down there?"

"No, I was following Reg's orders, Flori. He wanted me to check out the house. I told you we were working together to solve this murder, didn't I?"

"Well, I'll have Jake talk to Reg about that. There's no way he's going to get you to go into dangerous places anymore. He's sending you in so he doesn't have to go. And, sending a woman? That's plain sinful; that's what it is."

"No, Flori, whatever you do, don't talk to Jake. It's no big deal. He didn't send me in because I'm a woman. Now, I want you to go home and go back to bed. Don't forget, I have to go to work tomorrow and I really need to sleep."

"Oh, I'm so sorry. I am being selfish, aren't I? You've had a terrible day and I should let you sleep and recover. I'll bring a treat over to the shop in the morning to have with our coffee."

"Thanks, Flori, you're a sweetheart. I knew you'd understand."

She stood up.

"We'll discuss the gin in the morning too."

I didn't reach for my gin and tonic until after I heard Flori yell up that she was locking the door. I picked the glass up and stared at it. There were about three swallows left. I looked down at the floor. Nothing had spilled.

A slightly inebriated orange and white cat sat looking up at me. She blinked several times, yawned, and without doing her usual turnabout, sank to the floor. I wasn't exactly sure what I should do but since most drunks just need to sleep it off, I thought I'd give that a go.

I was too lazy to wash and refill my drink so I put the glass on the table, shut the light off and listened to Daisy snore until I fell asleep.

Chapter Thirty Eight

Daisy was still snoring when a loud crack on the window jolted me out of my sleep. It sounded like a shotgun going off. I jumped out of bed making sure whoever was outside couldn't see me as I inched toward the window. I was about to peek around my curtain when there was another sharp smacking sound on the glass. By now, I was awake enough to realize a bullet would've went through the glass. I looked down below.

Charlie Thompson was standing below my window, looking up. I opened the window.

"Charlie, what are you doing down there?"

"You have to come, Mabel."

I glanced at the clock. It was ten after three.

"Couldn't it wait until morning? I just got to sleep."

He shook his head. It was a good thing that the moon was so bright because knowing Charlie, he might not speak again.

"Okay, wait there. I'll be right down."

I slipped my jeans over my nightgown and shoved my feet into my runners. No socks and no underwear but who would see me running around Parson's Cove at this time of night?

Three cats went out the door as soon as I opened it and I did not intend to chase after them. I ran around the corner of the house and almost knocked Charlie over.

"What's the matter, Charlie? Don't tell me you found a body or something like that."

Charlie didn't say a word; he just took off at a very brisk walk. With my short legs, I almost had to run to keep up. Whatever was so important was down by the lake because that seemed to be where we were heading. We reached the beach and he kept walking down towards his house.

By this time, I was starting to huff and puff. "Are we almost there?" I asked.

Charlie stopped so suddenly in front of me that I smacked into him. He didn't speak; just stood there, so I carefully craned my neck around his body. Someone was sitting on the beach. I couldn't make out who it was until I heard the voice.

"Charlie," I whispered. "That's Murray down there. He's saying the Lord's prayer. Why did you come to get me? Erma should be with him."

Charlie shook his head. "She wouldn't answer the door." He turned to face me. "See if you can help, Mabel. He didn't do it."

"He didn't do what?" But it was too late. As soon as Charlie uttered the last sentence, he disappeared up the bank and was gone. I turned to face Murray, the moment Murray looked up and saw me.

"Mabel," he said. "What are you doing here?"

The moonlight was bright enough to show the tears running down his face.

I walked up to him but cautiously because I remembered our last encounter.

"Murray, I'm your friend. Charlie is, too. He saw you down here and he was worried. He came to tell me because I'm about the only friend he has. He didn't know what else to do."

Murray's hand trembled as he wiped his cheeks. He'd changed so much during the past few days that I might've walked by him on the street and thought it was a stranger.

He looked very vulnerable so without any thought of danger, I sat down beside him.

"What's going on, my friend?" I said. "You are not yourself. Erma is very worried about you."

He looked over at me. "Erma isn't worried about me. She thinks that I killed Bernie."

"No, I'm sure she doesn't. She's your wife and she loves you, Murray. She got some pills from Fritzy to help you sleep. I know she doesn't think that you killed Bernie. Why would she think that?"

"Because Bernie killed Biscuit so she thinks I killed Bernie because of that."

"Bernie killed Biscuit? Are you sure? Why would he do that?"

Murray sighed and a few more tears spilled out.

"On that day, Erma took Biscuit for a walk. She never took him for a walk but she did that day. She was across from Krueger's old house when Biscuit ran after Bernie and started biting his shoes. He pulled one right off his foot and started shaking it. Apparently, Bernie got so mad that he ran and picked up a brick and hit Biscuit with it."

"Why didn't you tell the police this, Murray?"

"Erma told me not to tell anyone. She said that if I did, it would look very suspicious for me. I'd have the motive and the brick was by my house. It's the same brick that someone used to kill Bernie."

I patted him on the back. "Murray, no one would suspect you. Besides, the police have to have proof. The cops from the city are gone but I think, in the morning, you'd better go and have a talk with Reg. You can't go on like this; you'll have some sort of breakdown."

"I'm not having a breakdown. It's those pills Erma is giving me. I feel drugged all the time and feel like life isn't worth living. This is the first time in my life that I've ever had suicidal thoughts." He grabbed my hand.

"This isn't me. I felt bad about my dog but I didn't need all these drugs to cope." His hand tightened on mine. "I mean it, Mabel, it's the pills."

"When did Erma start giving them to you?"

He rubbed his temple with his hands. "I think it was before Biscuit was killed. First, she told me they were for my allergies. Then, afterwards, she admitted that they were for my nerves. Then, she said some were vitamins. She was afraid I'd crack up when I heard about Biscuit so she made sure I took something before I found out."

"Are you telling me that she ran over to Doc's clinic to get these pills before Biscuit was even dead?"

He looked confused. "I don't understand this. Why would she do that?"

I smiled at him. "Murray, Erma loves you so much. I think she's a little over-protective. You'll have to forgive her for that. If I were you, I'd go into your gazebo in the back yard and try to get some sleep. You don't want to disturb Erma, do you?"

He shook his head. "I won't disturb Erma; she took off earlier to go to visit her mother in Chicago."

"Really? Well, you head right back to bed then and don't worry about anything. Everything will be sorted out in the morning."

A smile crossed his face. "Thanks. You called me your friend, Mabel, and I know that you are."

I don't think I'm getting soft in my old age but I couldn't help wrapping my arms around Murray.

I watched for a few minutes to make sure he was walking in the right direction and then I raced off to Doc Fritz's house. It must've been close to four by now but it didn't matter anyway.

I think Fritz' wife's name is Gloria. I should know it. I mean, we're a small town where everyone knows everyone. However, not that many people know Gloria.

Patty, who publishes the Parson's Cove Weekly, says she's a recluse and not only that, a hoarder. Well, I don't believe everything Patty says but in this case, I do.

When they arrived about five years ago, they bought the house closest to the hospital. At least, the closest one that was for sale. It's an old monstrosity of a place and every generation of kids believes that it's haunted. My generation included.

Since old emotions never seem to leave a person entirely, I opened the gate and walked up the pathway with some trepidation. The silver moon cast an eerie glow over everything. The house stood towards the back of the street with large shade trees surrounding it. If I heard any sound at all now, I would simply die from fright. I had too many memories of going up this path on a dare and someone letting out a high-pitched scream as I reached for the doorknob.

I picked up the doorknocker and rapped the wooden door with it. I decided to keep this up until Fritz answered. After banging it for at least twenty times, I decided to try something different. I found the doorknob and turned it. The door opened.

"Fritzy," I yelled into the darkness. "Are you home?"

From somewhere within the house, I heard the patter of feet and within seconds, the doctor stood staring at me. He moved his hand and lights went on.

Doc Fritz stood before me in baby blue pajamas with fuzzy blue slippers on his feet.

"Mabel," he said, with a bewildered look on his face, "What are you doing here?"

"Doc," I said. "I apologize for waking you up but this is very important. Did you give Erma McFerguson pills for Murray? Do you remember? It's important in solving a murder and I have to know before the murderer disappears in the streets of Chicago."

"Well, that does sound important. We certainly wouldn't want a murderer running loose in Chicago, would we? Miss Wickles, I'll have you know that I am not a pill pusher. I have never spoken to Erma McFerguson nor have I prescribed any drugs for her husband. I have no idea where you would get such an idea."

"Thank you so much. You can go back to bed now. I won't bother you again."

My next stop was Sheriff Smee's house and he was not as easy to awaken from sleep as Fritzy. Finally, after knocking, ringing the bell at the front door and throwing stones at the windows, he came to the door.

"Boy, Reg, if there were ever an emergency around here, you are definitely the last person I would try to contact. I've been standing here for at least ten minutes."

"Actually, Mabel, I did hear you but I thought it was just some punk kids playing pranks. Okay, so it's you. What do you want?"

"What do I want? I want to tell you who killed Bernie Bernstein, that's what I want to tell you."

Chapter Thirty Nine

Four days later, with a smile as wide as the Mississippi in springtime, Sheriff Reg Smee entered my shop. It was 9:06 to be exact. I know because I looked up at the clock wondering who was opening my door so early in the morning.

"Well, Mabel," he said. "The carwash murder is all wrapped up! The mystery is solved; thanks to a very bright amateur sleuth and a very discerning small town sheriff."

I imagine my smile matched the sheriff's smile. "Sheriff, let's celebrate with a cup of freshly brewed coffee and a slightly stale apple muffin."

"Stale?"

"Don't sound so disappointed. You know my muffins are always delicious. Sit down and I'll start you off with your coffee. Meanwhile, you get all your thoughts straight so you can tell me exactly what happened."

In less than five minutes, we were sitting facing each other, coffee in hand.

"Okay, Reg. Was I right? Did Erma kill Bernie?"

"Yes, you were right." He took a bite of muffin.

"What about Biscuit? Who killed Biscuit?"

He swallowed and washed everything down with a big gulp of coffee.

"Can I finish eating first?"

There were three more muffins on the plate. He held half of one in his hand.

"Of course, you can." I picked up the plate and took it to the back room.

"Hey! I might want more than one muffin, you know."

I sat back down again. "And you may have more than one after you tell me the whole story, Reg."

Reg laughed. "You're a tough one, Mabel, but since you probably did the most work solving the case, I guess you should get to know all the details."

"Yes, I think I should. Now, start from the beginning. What exactly happened the day that Bernie was murdered?"

Reg cleared his throat and took another drink of coffee.

"I guess we should go back to how Bernie was involved in all of this. He found out about the drugs and wanted in on it. You remember he got the wrong pair of boots from Scooter. Jeff told him that he would let him deal some but he couldn't interfere with the thing they had going at the nursing home. Bernie found a few teenagers who wanted to try it out so he'd meet them behind the carwash."

"So, there was a reason for going there besides washing the hub caps on his car."

"Yep. It was mostly to deal a few drugs. So happened that one night Erma spotted him down at the beach with Jeff and a couple of kids. She started questioning Melanie about Bernie so it didn't take long to put everything together. I think she was getting a little bored now that Murray was home all the time. She wanted to travel but all he wanted to do was to go fishing or sit all day at the café so she decided to have some excitement on her own; in addition to making some cash. She used Biscuit as an excuse to walk down to the Krueger house to see Jeff. Bernie's car was parked on the street and wouldn't you know it – you were right, Mabel, that old dog went crazy when he smelled those tires. Bernie heard the dog barking and saw Erma trying to pull the dog away so he went out. Of course, he'd just filled the hollow in his boots with drugs so Biscuit attacked his foot. He ripped the boot apart and drugs flew all over. This got Bernie into a rage so he grabbed the nearest weapon, which happened to be a brick off that old pile, and he went at Biscuit. When he was finished Biscuit was dead and Erma was terrified to think what Murray would say."

"What about Biscuit? She didn't feel anything for the dog?"

He shrugged. "I don't know. Doesn't seem like it. She always thought Murray cared more for the old dog than for her anyway."

"Well, I'm beginning to see why. What did they decide to do?"

"Bernie told her to hide the brick and he'd hide the dog. She would tell Murray that the dog ran off and she didn't know where he went."

"So he threw the dog in the field, not thinking that anyone would find the poor animal right away."

He nodded. "It wasn't long and those boys found Biscuit. They knew whose dog it was, so took him to Murray's house."

"Murray said that Erma was starting to give him drugs before Biscuit was killed though. Why would she do that?"

"She claims she would never have hurt him but I think she was hoping that if she gave Murray enough drugs for a long period of time, he might eventually take his own life or be so drugged up that he'd have some sort of accident."

"You're right. Murray said those pills gave him suicidal thoughts. But why did Erma kill Bernie?"

"She was so mad that he threw the dog in the field and didn't bury him someplace so no one would find him. Don't forget, there wasn't much time between Bernie killing Biscuit and Erma killing Bernie. Two hours at the most. She hid the brick by a tree. She was going to throw it into the lake but there were some boats close by so she couldn't. While Murray was mourning his dog and wondering why the dog would ever leave Erma's side, she ran out to throw the brick in the lake. When she got down there, she saw Melanie and Bernie fighting. As soon as Melanie ran away, she went after Bernie. He was still struggling to get out of the water; otherwise, she probably wouldn't have been able to hit him like that."

"Where did they find Erma anyway? Did she get all the way to Chicago?"

He laughed. "Wouldn't you know, all the flights were booked but when she finally got one, her plane was delayed so she never even got out of the Airport. Captain Maxymowich and his gang picked her up with no incident. Apparently, she did claim her innocence at the beginning but when she realized they knew Dr. Fritz hadn't prescribed any drugs for Murray, she broke down and confessed. Good work, Mabel."

I smiled. "We owe all of that to Charlie, Reg. He's the one who woke me up at three in the morning and told me to get over there. If it weren't for him, Erma would be in Chicago now. Of course, Sammy and Biscuit have to get some credit too. After all, if it weren't for their good sense of smell, we might not have realized where those drugs were hiding. Too bad we can't give a posthumous award to Biscuit."

"Maybe we could get something made up for Murray. You know a plaque with Biscuit's name on it. I think he'd really like that. He doesn't have too much to live for right now and that would cheer him up. What do you think, Mabel?"

I was seeing my sheriff in a new light. "I think that's a wonderful idea. By the way, what's happening with Prunella? Did she ever confess that someone hit her with the frying pan or is she still saying that she fell and hit her head?"

"I almost forgot to tell you about that. Melanie's brother, Steven, came into the station yesterday and confessed. He's another hothead. Once he found out that Melanie wasn't a murder suspect and that Erma was arrested, he decided to come forward. He'd wanted Prunella to say that she'd been wrong when she heard Melanie threatening Bernie's life. After all, Prunella's statement was very damaging."

"So he planted money and drugs in her drawer and put drugs in her booze so we'd think she was using. If that were true, the police would question her statement and probably not accept it, right?"

"That's right."

"Well, we can all give a sigh of relief now. Parson's Cove is back to normal."

"Not quite, Mabel."

"What do you mean, 'not quite'?"

"I heard via the grapevine that there's going to be a wedding coming up soon."

"A wedding? Reg, you know I don't know any of the young people in Parson's Cove anymore. It really doesn't interest me too much."

Reg grinned. "I think this one might. You know the bride quite well. In fact, she's a regular customer of yours."

I couldn't think of any customer of mine who would be even eligible for marriage. "Sorry, Reg. It can't be any of my customers. You'll have to tell me."

"Esther Flynn is marrying some old bachelor from Betula."

I don't remember much of the next ten minutes. I do remember Reg waving a newspaper in front of me and asking if I could hear him. Reality did finally click in.

"Well, you're right. Parson's Cove is definitely not ever going to be back to normal."

"Something else. There's going to be an election coming up within the next few weeks."

"There is? Well, since I've never voted in my lifetime, I'm not too concerned. I don't think it will make any difference to our small town."

"I don't know. Getting a new sheriff always means a few changes."

I stared at him. "A new sheriff? Are you telling me that you are really and truly retiring, Reg Smee?"

He grinned. "I handed in my resignation two days ago. It's time for me to spend some time fishing and relaxing before I settle down in the Parson's Cove Restful Retirement Retreat."

I reached over and shook his hand. "Congratulations, Reg. I'm happy for you but I don't think we will ever have a sheriff as good as you again."

"What? Is this the real Mabel Wickles speaking?"

"I know we've had our differences, Reg, but in the end, we work pretty well together."

There was a bit of shine to the sheriff's eyes. "We do, Mabel. I have to confess I'll miss our little adventures."

"Of course, no one is saying we still can't do some investigating once in a while. And, as you pointed out, Sheriff, when you're a citizen you don't even need a search warrant."

Reg laughed so hard, I had to grab his cup before it hit the floor. He wiped away a few tears and said, "Mabel, why don't you get me another one of your stale muffins?"

"Only as long as you're sheriff; once you're retired, you have to get your own."

The End

Flori's Cinnamon Buns

Makes 8 good-sized buns or 6 gargantuan buns!
Preparation and cook time: 1 hour 45 minutes.
Ingredients:
2 cups of white flour
1 tbsp. ground cinnamon
½ cup fine sugar
½ cup light brown sugar
Pinch of salt
1 cup chopped pecans
1 oz. butter
½ cup butter, melted
¼ oz. yeast
2 oz. maple syrup
1 egg, beaten
½ cup pecans, chopped
½ cup warm milk

Put flour, sugar, and salt in mixing bowl, blend in butter until the mixture resembles breadcrumbs. Stir in the yeast, egg, and milk and mix well until it forms a soft dough. Turn onto lightly floured surface and knead for ten minutes until smooth and elastic. Place the dough in a lightly oiled bowl and cover with a tea towel or plastic wrap. Leave in a warm place for 1 hour or until doubled in size. Combine the cinnamon, sugar, and pecans in a food processor until the nuts are finely ground.

Punch down the dough and knead to remove the air. Roll on a floured surface to form 9 in. X 12 in. rectangle. Brush the dough with half the melted butter and sprinkle over the sugar, cinnamon, and pecans. Roll up the dough tightly, starting at longer edge. Press the edges to seal, then cut into 8 slices. Grease pan (or pans) with butter. Put buns in pans, cover, and leave in a warm place for 30 minutes or until doubled in size.

Heat oven to 375* F. Bake for 30 minutes until golden. Remove from oven and place on rack to cool.

Heat the maple syrup, sugar, and remaining melted butter in a saucepan, stirring. Drizzle the glaze over the buns and sprinkle with pecans.

Mabel's Apple Breakfast Muffins

Makes 12 muffins
Preparation and cook time: 35 minutes

Bake 15 to 20 minutes in 375*F oven
Ingredients:
1 oz. butter
1 tsp. apple pie spice
1 oz. demerara sugar
2 apples, cored and cubed
1 oz. ground almonds
1 egg
2 oz. sunflower seeds
1 cup sour cream
2 cups all purpose flour
½ cup butter, melted
2 tsp. baking powder
½ cup brown sugar

Blend butter into flour, sugar, and almonds until mixture resembles breadcrumbs. Stir in sunflower seeds and set aside as topping. Sift flour and baking powder into mixing bowl. Stir in sugar, spice, and apple. Mix together egg, sour cream, and melted butter. Mix the wet and dry ingredients together and stir lightly. Mixture should be lumpy. Spoon the mixture into paper lined muffin tins and sprinkle on topping.
Bake until muffins are well risen and firm.

Flori's Chocolate-chocolate Cookies
1 ¼ cups flour
1 (4 serving size) chocolate instant pudding
1 tsp. soda
2 eggs
1 cup margarine, softened
1 (12 oz.) pkg. chocolate chips
¼ cup sugar
1 cup chopped nuts, optional
¾ cup brown sugar
1 tsp. vanilla

Mix flour with soda. Combine margarine, sugars, vanilla, and pudding mix in large bowl; beat until smooth and creamy. Beat in eggs. Add flour mixture. Stir in nuts and chips. Drop by teaspoonful onto ungreased sheets. 375* for about 8 to 10 minutes. Makes about 7 dozen small cookies.

ABOUT THE AUTHOR

Sharon Rose and her husband, Al, (now retired) live in the home that they designed and built over thirty years ago in a small community in Manitoba, Canada. Sharon squeezes in writing time between volunteering and grandchildren's visits. Every winter, she and her husband escape the cold northern winds and head for Galveston, Texas.

While taking a three-year writing course with the Writing School in Ottawa, Canada, she had two novels published.  One of her short stories appeared in *Woman's World*. Since then, she's had several short stories and one children's story published. Her real love, however, is writing cozy mysteries involving her two favorite characters: Mabel Wickles and Flori Flanders. Their first adventure was SLIP AND GO DIE and the second was PERPLEXITY ON P 1/2. This is her third Parson's Cove mystery.

You can contact Sharon at her author website: www. sharonrosemierke.weebly.com

16476524R00146

Made in the USA
Charleston, SC
22 December 2012